"I'M NOT READY FOR ANY CHANGES IN MY LIFE," JENNIE SAID UNHAPPILY.

"You mean you're not willing to take the risk of caring for someone," Matt challenged.

"I need more time. It isn't fair to you if—"

"I'll decide that," he said firmly, his dark brown eyes holding her gaze.

"Will you let me finish a sentence?"

"No, I don't think so. Jennie, I'm thirty-two and I've never been married. Do you think I'm going to rush into a relationship just because you're beautiful, sweet, and sexy?"

Was he teasing? "You're making it hard—"

He took her into his arms. "For you to get rid of me? I sure hope so. . . ."

CANDLELIGHT ECSTASY CLASSIC ROMANCES

THE TAWNY GOLD MAN, *Amii Lorin*
GENTLE PIRATE, *Jayne Castle*

CANDLELIGHT ECSTASY ROMANCES®

450 SWEET REVENGE, *Tate McKenna*
451 FLIGHT OF FANCY, *Jane Atkin*
452 THE MAVERICK AND THE LADY, *Heather Graham*
453 NO GREATER LOVE, *Jan Stuart*
454 THE PERFECT MATCH, *Anna Hudson*
455 STOLEN PASSION, *Alexis Hill Jordan*

QUANTITY SALES

Most Dell Books are available at special quantity discounts when purchased in bulk by corporations, organizations, and special-interest groups. Custom imprinting or excerpting can also be done to fit special needs. For details write: Dell Publishing Co., Inc., 1 Dag Hammarskjold Plaza, New York, NY 10017, Attn.: Special Sales Dept., or phone: (212) 605-3319.

INDIVIDUAL SALES

Are there any Dell Books you want but cannot find in your local stores? If so, you can order them directly from us. You can get any Dell book in print. Simply include the book's title, author, and ISBN number, if you have it, along with a check or money order (no cash can be accepted) for the full retail price plus 75¢ per copy to cover shipping and handling. Mail to: Dell Readers Service, Dept. FM, P.O. Box 1000, Pine Brook, NJ 07058.

TRAPPED BY DESIRE

Barbara Andrews

A CANDLELIGHT ECSTASY ROMANCE®

Published by
Dell Publishing Co., Inc.
1 Dag Hammarskjold Plaza
New York, New York 10017

Copyright © 1986 by Barbara Andrews

All rights reserved. No part of this book may be reproduced or transmitted in any form or by any means, electronic or mechanical, including photocopying, recording or by any information storage and retrieval system, without the written permission of the Publisher, except where permitted by law.

Dell ® TM 681510, Dell Publishing Co., Inc.

Candlelight Ecstasy Romance®, 1,203,540, is a registered trademark of Dell Publishing Co., Inc., New York, New York.

ISBN: 0-440-19056-8

Printed in the United States of America

September 1986

10 9 8 7 6 5 4 3 2 1

WFH

To Our Readers:

We have been delighted with your enthusiastic response to Candlelight Ecstasy Romances®, and we thank you for the interest you have shown in this exciting series.

In the upcoming months we will continue to present the distinctive sensuous love stories you have come to expect only from Ecstasy. We look forward to bringing you many more books from your favorite authors and also the very finest work from new authors of contemporary romantic fiction.

As always, we are striving to present the unique, absorbing love stories that you enjoy most—books that are more than ordinary romance. Your suggestions and comments are always welcome. Please write to us at the address below.

      Sincerely,

      The Editors
      Candlelight Romances
      1 Dag Hammarskjold Plaza
      New York, New York 10017

TRAPPED BY DESIRE

CHAPTER ONE

The soles of her new penny loafers were slippery as Jennie ran up the seven steps from her basement apartment, so she scraped them on the cement walk a few times before crossing the damp grass to the front of the building. There, beside her ground-level living-room window, was the first sign of spring: a bright-purple crocus that had, almost overnight, pushed through the dark earth beside the brick wall. She'd been the first tenant in the twelve-unit building to plant her own bulbs, mostly tulips and daffodils, but now the walkways and strips of soil along the walls would be a riot of color in late spring, lovingly tended by nearly half of the building's residents.

The winter had been long and cold in Burdick, Michigan; the last of the snow lingered in shadowed places, under bushes and in window wells, until the icy deposits were as gritty as the dirt around them. Wanting to welcome the new season with touch as well as sight, Jennie stooped and pulled off one tan leather glove, delicately fingering the amazing conical flower. As much as she enjoyed plants, filling every spot the sun could touch in her home with shiny, green-leafed vegetation, she loved best the flowers that grew outside, always glad the dogwood and lilac blossoms were left on the great bushes scattered around the apartment complex. Once cut, blooms died, and she didn't like the wilted stalks they became after a few days. They reminded her of what she most wanted to forget: death.

She stood, impatient with herself for harboring morbid thoughts, and smoothed her bulky navy sweater down over slender hips, deciding her tan wool slacks and pert navy beret, covering one side of her ash-blond, chin-length hair, would provide sufficient warmth on this crisp Saturday morning. After pulling on her glove she secured the strap of a big leather pouch on her shoulder and started walking toward the downtown business district.

It was far too lovely a day for gloom, and she didn't want to spend it mourning for Kirk. She had an important errand; buying a gift. Martha Berry, the head of the claims department of Safeguard Health Insurance where Jennie worked, was retiring, and everyone in the large department had given generously for a going-away present. Jennie had been designated to buy something very special for the popular supervisor. The contributions amounted to a substantial sum, enough to prompt her to deposit the money in her account for safekeeping and pay by check when she made a selection. Her plan was to ask the store to hold the gift for a few days so people in the office could see it if they wished before a final purchase was made.

"You don't need to do that," her best friend at work, Tonya Willis, had said. "Everyone knows you have marvelous taste. Look at the way you dress. And on our salary!"

The secret of Jennie's wardrobe was simple: she shopped fabric sales and made most of her own clothes, filling empty evenings with the comforting hum of her sewing machine. Since her roommate had married nearly a year ago, she'd converted the second bedroom to a sewing room, sometimes working up patterns for others to augment her none-too-generous salary.

The walk downtown to her destination, Garber's Jewelry, was a long one, but being outside in the spring air was invigorating. Jennie spent too much time riding the lumbering red-and-white city buses, breathing foul exhaust, and vying for a seat. On a day like this she could almost believe her life was going somewhere; it hadn't ended when a doctor in hospital greens broke the news of her young husband's death on an operating table.

After a few blocks the tightness in her calves disappeared, letting her walk at a fast pace. She felt taller than her five feet three inches, and the brisk air was bringing a lovely color to cheeks that had often been pallid in the last three years. Jennie felt so buoyed by the promise of spring that a trio of motorcycles speeding by as she waited for a traffic signal brought only a ghost of a frown.

Shopping was one of her real pleasures, and she wanted to do an especially good job in choosing a gift for Martha. The older woman had been helpful and understanding on many occasions, and Jennie respected and admired her. The most frequent suggestion around the office had been a watch, one Martha could wear to concerts and theater performances instead of her practical everyday one. Jennie had already checked out other stores during her lunch breaks, and last Saturday she'd visited a large mall on the outskirts of town. Garber's had the best selection by far, which was nice because, without a car, it was more convenient to shop in downtown Burdick.

The jeweler had been open less than ten minutes, and only one other early-bird was waiting for service in the elegant, blue-carpeted interior. High display windows curved out on either side of the entrance. At night a modern security grill descended over the whole front, but this morning the store had a solid, traditional appearance with glass display cases on three sides and a huge crystal chandelier hanging from the center of a metal-tiled ceiling. Unlike newer stores Garber's refused to clutter their display area with souvenir plates, ceramic figurines, or knickknacks of any description. They sold fine jewelry and watches; a gift box with their name was a guarantee of quality. As a lifelong resident of the city Martha would appreciate this more than Jennie, who'd only moved there from her small hometown of Hopewell, Indiana, to live with a friend after Kirk's death.

Peering into the glass case she knew exactly which watch she'd choose to wear herself: a Swiss make with a delicate oval face in a textured gold setting, the solid band fitting like a bracelet. But she had to keep in mind her supervisor's preference for bolder jewelry. Martha might prefer the square face surrounded by diamond chips. No, that was too gaudy. Jennie looked up to see if a clerk could show her one of the trays and met instead the very direct gaze of the other customer.

She'd heard him speak to a silver-haired woman behind the counter, something about picking up an engagement ring left for sizing, but his intent stare caught her by surprise. A fleeting glance was enough to set off her personal alarm system. He was handsome, with sable-brown hair brushed casually over a high forehead, and a winning grin that revealed white, even teeth; just the type of man who might appeal to her if she weren't determined to avoid relationships. With no desire to flirt, certainly not with a man who was picking up an engagement ring, she turned away and looked out through one of the front windows. Jennie could almost feel a pair of dark-brown eyes following her, although she surprised herself by having noticed his eye color on a casual glance, something she rarely did.

Really, she was being silly! she thought as she noticed a young man walking toward the entrance. If he hadn't been so shabby, his Windbreaker soiled to a muddy brown shade, she might not have given him a second, more curious glance. He didn't look as if he could afford to buy one of Garber's empty gift-boxes, let alone shop for expensive jewelry.

Before she knew what was happening, Jennie saw him pull a black-and-yellow ski mask from his jacket pocket and yank it over his head. Then he rushed into the store.

14

Closing the door by slamming his shoulder against it, he lowered the shade and pulled something from under his Windbreaker.

"This is a gun! Everybody down on the floor!"

A man came into the shop from the rear, took in what was happening, and reacted instantly, putting his hands above his head and telling the others, "Do as he says!" Then turning to the gunman, said, "We won't give you any trouble."

"You! Out in the middle." The young man waved the gun nervously, gesturing at all four people in the store to drop to the floor.

Too shocked to do anything else, Jennie collapsed to her knees and then, at another shrill command from the man with the gun, sank forward on her face, hands stretched above her head. It took a moment to realize the pounding she heard was her own heart, and her body stiffened with dread, expecting at any moment to hear a lethal shot from the weapon.

The others obeyed too. He didn't shout again. Instead an explosive crackling noise shattered the unnatural silence as he smashed one of the display cases, the one filled with rings. Would he steal the other customer's engagement ring? It was a crazy thing to worry about, but Jennie didn't want him to lose it, even if he was something of a flirt.

She was lying with her head toward the back of the store, the carpet scratching her chin, her eyes squeezed shut as though she could block out what was happening. Would an alarm sound at police headquarters when the case was broken, or was that too much to hope for?

Deciding the thief was too busy stealing to notice, she cautiously opened one eye and then the other, moving her head very, very slowly to the side to get her nose and chin away from the floor. Suddenly the man backed away from the case, his heel coming down so hard on her outstretched fingers she cried aloud, terrifying herself because she'd risked attracting his attention. His feet were dirty, she saw, with thin white ankles sticking out of grimy blue sneakers. *He should wear socks,* she thought inanely, fighting back panic by concentrating on the line of dried blood where he'd cut himself.

"If anyone moves for five minutes, you're dead!" His voice was shrill, sounding as frightened as she felt. The buzzer that announced customers sounded as he opened the door, then forced it shut against the pressure of the door closer.

His threat had to be a desperate ploy to gain time; he couldn't run away and be there to shoot them, but it took several long moments for the shock to wear off enough for people to stir.

"The police are on the way," the male jeweler said. "I managed to step on our alarm button. He was an amateur." His sigh was as loud as his words. "They can be the most dangerous."

Dragging herself to a sitting position Jennie wasn't sure she could stand.

"Here, let me help you."

She took the hand that was offered, smiling weakly but gratefully at the other customer.

"Are you all right?"

"Yes, I think so." She tentatively wiggled her fingers; they hurt, but not enough to be broken. "He stepped on my hand, but it startled me more than anything else."

The man took her hand in his, laying her outstretched fingers on his palm, studying them with a troubled frown.

"They're fine, really." She took her hand away, blaming her new feeling of confusion on the robbery.

"Some excitement!" He smiled warmly. "I'm Matt Nichols."

"Thank you, Mr. Nichols." She wasn't sure whether

thanks were in order, then remembered he had helped her up.

"Matt. And you're?"

"Jennie Martin."

"You are sure you're all right?"

She nodded.

The two silver-haired clerks, who turned out to be the married couple who owned the store, were conferring urgently behind the counter, trying to make a quick estimate of their loss while comforting each other.

"At least no one was hurt," the woman said fervently. "I'm Emma Garber. This is my husband Nelson. You two are all right, aren't you?"

The police arrived before they could exchange reassurances, the uniformed officers quickly taking charge, several leaving in pursuit while one phoned police headquarters and another started questioning the four of them.

Not since the night of Kirk's crash had Jennie been so close to this many policemen. Their uniforms and holstered guns, the tools of their profession, set them apart from other men. Courteous, matter of fact, personable, they still triggered old dreads, reminding her of all the terrible waits spent wondering if her husband's obsession with racing his motorcycle would lead to disaster. Eventually it had.

"I saw him put it on just outside the door. You did too, didn't you, Jennie?" Matt asked.

"What?"

Embarrassed because she hadn't been paying attention at such a crucial time, she didn't even notice that the man she'd just met had used her first name as though they were old friends.

"Did you see the thief before he put on the ski mask?" one of the officers asked.

Until that moment she'd forgotten that she had.

"Yes," she agreed, trying to recreate the scene in her

mind. "He stopped just outside the door. It was in his pocket."

"Can you describe him?"

"He was young."

"A juvenile?"

"No, but under twenty, I think."

"Hair?" The man's rapid-fire technique of questioning wasn't helping her remember.

"Dark. Brown, I think."

"Any distinguishing characteristics?"

"He was shabby. His jacket was really dirty—sort of a muddy brown. His face was long, I'd say, and his hair fell over his forehead, not like . . ." She looked at the other customer and could only remember his first name. "Matt's."

"Clean shaven?"

"He had some whiskers on his face, like he hadn't shaved in a day or two. Oh, and his chin was kind of pointy."

"Complexion?"

"Nothing unusual. Some acne, I think. Yes, that's why I thought he was young."

"Dark, olive, sallow, tanned?" the policeman prodded.

"Sallow, I suppose. No one's tan this time of year."

"So, only the two of you saw his face." He included Matt in his statement. "I'd like to have you come down to headquarters with me now."

"I don't know anything else." Jennie wasn't protesting; she just didn't see what she could add to her identification.

"One of the detectives will want to talk to you, then have you look at some mug shots and give your description to a police artist." His voice made it all sound very routine, but for her it wasn't.

"I want to cooperate, but this doesn't seem real."

"It's real, all right," the policeman said grimly. "You're lucky he didn't lose his head and start shooting."

"There's nothing else we could have done, then?" She was feeling very inadequate about the whole incident.

"You did exactly right," Matt said, stepping forward to reassure her. "This shouldn't take too long."

Matt helped her into the back of a black-and-white police car, sitting beside her and making small talk to take her mind away from the robbery. In a gray crew-neck sweater, hand-sewn moccasins, and faded jeans, he was dressed so casually she was surprised to learn he was a consultant with Hawkins-Davis, the town's largest investment firm.

Slowly, as she realized how close she'd been to death, a reaction set in, making Jennie shake just enough for him to detect it.

"You'll be all right," he assured her, taking one hand between his and gently massaging it, continuing to talk about inconsequential things: the fine weather, a concert scheduled in the park that spring, a building being demolished to make room for a new office building.

The only time she'd been inside the Burdick police station was when she'd applied for a Michigan driver's license, used for identification even though she couldn't afford to keep a car. Then she'd been in the wrong place; the licensing bureau wasn't in that building. Today felt wrong too; a morning that had started with finding the first crocus shouldn't end in this dreary place with institutional-green walls and scarred wood wainscoting and doors.

Detective Joe Woodbury was wearing brown polyester slacks and a herringbone wool jacket; the elbow patches had polished his desktop for most of his ten years in plain clothes. He was one of those people who look baby faced long after their hair turns white, and his was still salt and pepper. His deep voice, which didn't fit his pug nose and clear blue eyes, reminded Jennie of someone, but she wasn't sure who. He'd gone through his routine with witnesses so many times, the polite, carefully phrased words came out like a prerecorded statement.

Seated across from him at a varnished oak table in a small room, she repeated all she'd told the uniformed policemen. It didn't seem like much of a description when the police had to sift through a population of more than a hundred thousand for suspects.

"Do you remember which hand he used to hold the gun?"

She tried to visualize what he'd done from the time he reached for the gun in his jacket.

"I was standing to his left when he came through the door. That's the hand he used to take out the gun." She felt relieved she could remember a detail like that. "He must have been left handed."

The detective didn't comment on any of her answers; he just made notes on a legal-size yellow pad in front of him.

"Now, would you mind repeating your description to our artist?"

He led her to a tile-floored room. Matt Nichols was waiting there, ignoring several empty straight-backed chairs and standing with his fingers hooked into the back pockets of his jeans.

Instead of sketching on a pad the policeman acted more as a technician than an artist, building a face for them on the screen of a computer. Matt thought the thief's eyebrows were closer together; she was sure his chin was more sharply pointed. They agreed he was slender, with sunken cheeks and a rather poor complexion. Both were sure he'd held the gun in his left hand. Neither remembered which hand he'd used to put on the ski mask. Jennie thought it was both.

The two witnesses were finally dismissed at the same time; they'd been in the police station for several hours.

"I wouldn't want to do that every day," Matt said emphatically, holding the heavy door open for her.

"Me either! The more questions they asked, the more I remembered, but when they repeated the same ones over and over, I started doubting what I'd seen. It doesn't seem real."

"I know what you mean. After a while you don't think they believe you." He walked beside her down steep steps.

"I suppose so many people lie to them, they're skeptical of everything they hear," she said.

"That detective has a job I wouldn't want. My clients may get mad when the stock market goes down, but so far no one's tried to shoot me because silver dropped."

She laughed politely, still too tense to enjoy his easy sense of humor.

"Let me buy you a drink," he suggested casually.

"Oh, I don't think so, but thank you."

"You're right," he said congenially. "It's too early. If you don't mind walking back to my car, we can go to some nice quiet place far from the scene of the crime for lunch."

"Really, Mr. Nichols—"

"Matt," he insisted.

"Matt. I'm still a little shaky. I would like to go home."

"Someone waiting for you there?"

"No, but—"

"I think it'll do us both good to rehash this a little. I don't know about you, but this was my first armed robbery."

"Mine too!"

Suddenly talking about what had happened at the jewelry store seemed like a good idea. Jennie was too shaken to go back to an empty apartment, but wasn't ready to tell someone who hadn't been there. Tonya and her other friends would be enthralled by every detail, as if it were a great adventure, but Jennie wasn't calm enough to treat the robbery as a minor incident.

Matt put his hand on her elbow to indicate they should turn the corner.

"We can take a shortcut through the alley," he said. "Past the back of the bike shop."

"I thought that was a dead end."

"Not if we go in the back entrance of the drugstore and out the front. The pharmacist won't mind. I went to school with his son."

"You grew up here?"

"Born and bred," he said with a smile. "Have you lived here long?"

"About three years. I came from Indiana. You've probably never heard of the town: Hopewell."

"No, but I like the name. What do people do in Hopewell?"

"Sell things to farmers when they have any money. There's a plant that assembles campers too."

He opened what seemed to be a private entrance, walked through a passageway into the drugstore, and waved at a white-haired man with a long, droopy mustache who was counting out pills behind the prescription counter. The pharmacist smiled and called out a greeting without losing his count.

Back on the street Matt touched her shoulder, stepping to the outer side of the walk, something no one had done for her in ages. He was tall, a little over six feet, and moved with an easy grace. When his face was expressionless, he was a pleasant-looking man, not unusually handsome, but even-featured with a slightly prominent nose, lean cheekbones, and a strong chin with just a hint of a cleft dividing it.

"You will have lunch with me, won't you?" he asked hopefully, a warm smile transforming his face in an extraordinary way.

His eyes were dark brown with flecks of gold that made them seem to light up. Instead of creases running from the sides of his nose, he had smile lines that radiated sideways at an angle, forming a diamond with his broad grin, his square white teeth dazzling above a lower lip slightly fuller than the upper. His body, she noted, was lean and well-proportioned, from his square shoulders to his slender waist and hips and well-formed thighs outlined by tight jean legs.

"Well, maybe a cup of tea."

"There's my car. Oh, no! Can you believe it?" He rushed toward the front windshield of a tan Chevrolet and removed a pink slip stuck under the wiper.

"A parking ticket? That isn't fair!"

"I'm out serving the forces of law and order," he exclaimed, "and this is my reward."

They laughed because it was so ironic.

"You should send it to Detective Woodbury."

"The one with a voice like the Lone Ranger?"

"I knew he sounded familiar!"

"I expected to hear the *William Tell Overture* any moment," he said.

They laughed again because it felt good to be silly.

Matt drove to a white frame restaurant that had once been on the outskirts of town; but now the city had encroached on it, filling farmland with housing developments and building neighboring businesses on the other three corners. Still, Charlie's Roost had a country look with big green awnings and a collection of kitchen utensils inside the entrance.

"They have the best cole slaw in the world and the prettiest hostess," he said for the benefit of a waitress in a short calico dress and a red apron who came to show them to a table. She laughed and led the way to a cozy booth.

He was a flirt, Jennie decided, remembering his reason for being in the jewelry store and wishing she hadn't come. His engagement didn't matter to her; she had no intention of exposing herself to the pain of loving a man again. She just didn't want to be the cause of distress for his fiancée.

The lunch had better be a quick one; she'd insist on taking a cab home, even though it meant splurging on the fare.

Sitting in the quiet restaurant was a balm for her nerves, and Matt almost made her forget about the robbery, giving elaborate attention to the menu and telling her stories of hanging out in this same place when he was in high school.

"They're a lot fancier now," he said. "The tables used to have shiny black tops, and the chairs looked like they came from a fire sale. There were about twenty different kinds. I guess my generation made Charlie rich, hanging out here and eating double burgers with malts."

"Your generation? You make yourself sound ancient."

"Too old to still be a happy bachelor, my younger brother keeps telling me. It's his fault I was in on the robbery."

"How's that?" She looked up from the menu she'd been reading mainly to cover the awkwardness she felt being alone with an appealing man after such a long time.

"He's working in Detroit, but he ordered the ring for his fiancée at Garber's. I was picking it up this morning."

"Are you going to be his best man?" She was relieved that he wasn't engaged, although why she didn't know.

"Best brother, anyway. The only one he has. Do you come from a big family?"

"No, I only have one brother, Josh, but I hardly ever see him. He's career navy. Apt to turn up anywhere in the world, but fortunately his wife likes the life. I'm an aunt twice over, both little girls."

"I love kids," he said, telling her about the peewee hockey team he coached until a waitress interrupted to take their order.

"Have you decided?" he asked.

"Just hot tea, please."

"Not enough," he insisted. "You have to be famished after all that excitement. Do you like shrimp?"

"Yes, but—"

"Charlie makes the best shrimp plate in the world. Two," he said to the waitress, "with decaffeinated coffee for me."

"Do you always make up other people's minds for them?"

He smiled sheepishly.

"You probably feed stray cats too," she teased.

"It's impossible to look at you and think of a stray cat," he said sincerely.

Remember that he flirted with waitresses, too, she warned herself, wondering if there was something about a crisis situation that made people become friends very quickly.

"What were you looking for at Garber's?" he asked when they'd both finished a generous serving of shrimp in batter so light it melted on her tongue.

"My supervisor is retiring. I was elected to buy her a going-away present, maybe a watch."

"Our robber seemed to want rings."

"Did he steal your brother's?"

"No, Mrs. Garber dropped it and kicked it aside. Now, there's a couple who know how to keep their heads in an emergency!"

"Yes, they were marvelous. It's too bad neither of them saw him without a ski mask."

"Jennie," he said seriously, "you're not going to let this bother you, are you?"

"I can't help but wonder whether I'll recognize him if I see him again."

"Either you will or you won't. Worrying won't help."

"I know, but . . ." Her voice trailed off.

"You're a very nice person to be robbed with," he said.

"Thank you."

"There are probably easier ways to meet people," he joked, "but a holdup is certainly memorable."

"I really should leave now. I'll call for a ride from the pay phone across the street if they don't have one here."

"No need. I'll drive you home."

"You've already been too kind. I don't want to—"

"Trouble me? You'll only do that by refusing."

This time she intended to be firm.

Five minutes later she was in his car, telling him where she lived. It had been so long since anyone took little decisions out of her hands, she felt a bit steamrolled. He was a very nice person, sympathetic about the harrowing experience of the morning, and seemingly interested in everything she said. Grateful because he'd been there when she needed someone, she was just a tinge regretful that she wouldn't see him again. It was the wrong time to become interested in a man; she didn't know if it would ever be the right time.

"Is your name in the phone book?" he asked, stopping by the walkway that led to her apartment.

"Yes," she said, not mentioning it was listed as J. M. Martin, a single woman's defense against threatening calls. "Thank you for lunch and the ride."

"I'd like to call you," he said, touching her arm to keep her from leaving.

"It wouldn't be very"—she groped for a word—"convenient. Not right now."

Sliding off the car seat she didn't look back. Her apartment door was open before he pulled away from the curb.

Kicking off the stiff loafers, worn too long for a new pair of shoes, she sank down on the honey-colored corduroy couch without taking off her heavy sweater and hat. For a long time Jennie just sat and thought, trying to absorb everything that had happened. She'd been threatened at gunpoint, questioned by the police, and dined by an unusually nice man. Ordinarily she avoided crisis situations, not wanting to risk new emotional upheavals, but this one had been thrust on her. At least it was over, and they were just two people whose paths had crossed in an alarming way. Seeing more of Matt Nichols could only threaten her hard-won tranquility. Besides, she finally decided, there was only a small possibility he would call. They'd probably never see each other again, and that was the way it should be. Easily hurt and slow to heal, she wasn't going to risk her heart another time.

CHAPTER TWO

Leaving her dew-dampened shoes by the door, Tonya flopped down on one corner of the couch, wiggled a bit, then tucked her long, slender legs and stockinged feet under her, managing to curl her five feet ten inches into a cuddly position. She ran the fingers of one hand through tight red curls and studied her friend with inquisitive gray-green eyes.

"You mean the store was actually robbed? Boom, boom at gunpoint, just like on TV?"

"There wasn't any boom, but he made everyone lie face down on the floor."

"Why didn't you call me yesterday? I would have stayed the night with you," Tonya scolded, hugging knees clad in black sweat-pants. "Weren't you scared to death?"

"It happened so fast, I was more shocked than anything. Afterward I actually got the shakes."

"You shouldn't have been alone, Jennie."

"I wasn't, exactly. That is, I had lunch with the other witness. Talking it over helped."

"Imagine, you witnessed a crime. You'll have to testify at the trial."

"If they catch the robber. Things happened so fast! I wasn't even sure of my own name by the time the police got there."

"Oh, you're always so calm! You probably came home and worked on your dress for Martha's retirement party as if nothing had happened. I can't believe you didn't call me!"

"I didn't want to interfere with your date. You probably needed every minute to get ready after baby-sitting most of the day."

"No, my sister got home a little early, but even so I would have had more fun staying with the twins all evening. At age three they're better conversationalists than my date was."

"You didn't have fun?" Jennie asked. Tonya always got very excited about a first date with a new man, but she was often disappointed, either expecting too much or misjudging the person.

"We sat at a restaurant table three hours and thirty-seven minutes. I was sure they'd ask us to leave before he finished the story of his life. But tell me more about the robbery. Who's the other witness?"

"Just a man who happened to be in the store."

"Old, young, ugly, cute?"

"I think he said he's thirty-two. Certainly not ugly, but believe me, yesterday it didn't matter."

"It always matters! You never know, Jennie, someday you'll meet someone special. Was he tall?"

"Yes, over six foot, but I'm not looking for a man."

"Well, you should be. But leave the tall ones for me!"

"It's a deal. Do you want to jog some more? I'll go with you."

"You need to ask? On an afternoon like this, half the eligible bachelors in this city will be tramping through the park."

"With girl friends or children from their previous marriages," Jennie said wryly.

"Spoilsport! Let an old maid have her dreams."

"Old Maid is a card game. Let me get ready."

The phone in the kitchen rang while she was in the

bedroom trying to decide how to carry a key in running sweats with no pocket.

"I'll get it," Tonya called, uncoiling from the couch with an energetic burst that made her seem like a teenager although she was, at twenty-five, only two years younger than Jennie.

"I'll bet this one isn't selling magazine subscriptions," Tonya teased, holding her hand over the receiver as Jennie came to take it.

"Hello?" she answered absentmindedly until a familiar voice commandeered her full attention.

"Jennie, this is Matt Nichols. Have you recovered from the holdup?"

"Pretty much so, but I wouldn't want to go through another one. How are you?"

"Fine. I wondered if you'd like to have dinner with me tonight."

"Oh—thank you for asking, Matt, but I'm afraid I can't tonight."

"You have other plans?"

If she lied and said yes, it would encourage him to call again.

"No." She'd given her explanation many times before, but it seemed especially difficult this time. "Matt, I'm a widow, and I prefer not to go out with anyone. I should have told you yesterday."

"I see."

The disappointment in his voice made her uncomfortable. "Thank you for asking. Saying no doesn't mean I don't think you're a very nice person."

"How long since your husband . . ." He paused, searching for the delicate way to say 'died,' as people so often did.

"Not quite three years," she said quickly, disturbed because turning him down was proving so difficult.

"All I'm suggesting is dinner. We can talk some more about the robbery."

Men usually gave up immediately when she mentioned being a widow; dealing with grief wasn't anyone's idea of a good time. But Matt's persistence was making her feel defensive. Tightly gripping the phone receiver she was conscious of Tonya, who couldn't help but hear the conversation in the small apartment.

"I don't think so, thank you," she said, ending the call as quickly as possible.

Tonya's look rebuked her more emphatically than words.

"You're going to say I should go out with him."

"No, but I'm thinking it. Jennie, why not let yourself have a little fun?"

"I have fun. I'm as busy as I want to be."

"Yes, but all your friends are women!"

"Tonya," she said earnestly, needing her friend's understanding, "I like the way my life is now. It's calm and uneventful. I don't want romance to complicate it."

"I suppose you know what's best for yourself," her friend said, trying to hide her skepticism. "Let's jog."

Smiling gratefully Jennie followed her to the yard, where they did stretching exercises to prepare for a serious run. Tonya pretended jogging was only an excuse for a manhunt, but she took physical fitness seriously, making it enjoyable for Jennie to exercise with her.

They didn't talk about her dinner invitation again that afternoon, but it was constantly on Jennie's mind. It had been comforting to share the harrowing experience of the robbery with someone who was both involved and understanding; Matt helped put the incident in a sensible perspective, and for that she was grateful.

But it wouldn't be fair to let any man expect more from her than she could give. Her love had never been enough for Kirk, and even if the sorrow and loneliness stopped hurting, she still had to live with the fact that she hadn't been able to prevent his death. Their marriage had been too confining, too stifling, for her reckless young husband. The more she had tried to fulfill his expectations, the more he'd withdrawn from her, becoming obsessed with racing his motorcycle.

Jogging behind her friend, feeling the wind whip her hair against one cheek and hearing the satisfying slap of her soles on the pavement, Jennie tried to make her mind a blank, but the image of Kirk haunted her: his thick, sun-bleached hair covered by a heavy black helmet, his direct blue eyes concealed by the smoky visor. He'd farmed with his father for a living, but he'd lived to ride.

Alone in the big, gloomy country house vacated by his grandparents when they retired, hating the dark hours when the stalks of corn in the field across from their yard swayed in the wind like one giant living creature, she'd waited in fear and dread for the disaster that finally came. A sheriff's deputy came to tell her Kirk had crashed on the highway, taking one too many reckless chances cutting around a semi.

Jennie had known something bad would happen. There was nothing mystical or paranormal about her forebodings, but she had known. All her persuasiveness, all her love, had only driven him from the house more often. She was the only person who could have prevented his death. His parents hinted that she was partly to blame for his drinking and reckless racing; in the end, she agreed with them. Kirk was never happy with her; her concern and fear had only fueled his obsession with speed and danger.

Maybe, if she'd loved him less, she could have left him. But she stayed, a goad to his irresponsibility. Her love hadn't been enough. She wasn't going to risk feeling a crippling inadequacy again. The only sensible thing was to avoid getting involved.

Matt Nichols was far too likable. Even a casual friendship with him could be risky. Still, that didn't prevent her from thinking of him often during the next few days.

One evening she and Tonya went to a jewelry store in the mall and bought a watch for Martha's retirement. Jennie felt awkward about going back to Garber's, even though she admired the couple who ran the shop.

She wanted to put the trauma of the robbery behind her, but the police didn't let her. A call came at the office, requesting she come to headquarters during her lunch break to look at a lineup of suspects. Martha told her not to worry about getting back on time and insisted on driving her the ten blocks to the police station to save time.

"I'll be glad to wait, if you like," her supervisor offered, her brow creased with worry lines.

"No, it could take ages. I won't have you missing your lunch."

"You take time for something to eat before you come back to the office," the older woman insisted. "That's an order!"

His back was turned as he talked to a uniformed policeman, but she recognized Matt when she entered the station. His sable-brown hair looked even darker above the narrow rim of a white shirt collar, and the suit jacket that hugged broad shoulders and tapered to his slim waist and hips was the color of sunbaked sand. Expecting either hostility or indifference she tried to pass without being seen, but Matt turned toward her before she could do so.

"Jennie." He walked toward her smiling as pleasantly as he had when they went to lunch. "I thought you might be here too. Are you ready to look at the suspects?"

"If it's possible to be ready, I am. The robbery seems like something I dreamed."

"I know what you mean. It's something you don't expect to happen."

"I wonder if they've caught the right person."

"I imagine they expect us to tell them that."

A little tremor of nervousness passed through her, and she realized how reassuring it was that Matt had to identify the thief too. It was quite a responsibility to point out a man when her doing so could send him to jail. No matter how hard she tried, no clear picture of him came to mind. It hadn't occurred to Jennie to be afraid of the man himself, but she was scared of making a mistake.

Matt put his hand on the shoulder of her woven cotton rust-and-brown-striped jacket, worn over a simple cocoa-colored sheath, and guided her toward Detective Woodbury's office.

The lineup wasn't quite as dramatic as she'd expected, but there was a one-way window through which to view the suspects. There were four men, all young, with thin, hard faces and hair ranging from faded blond to mousy brown. The first man was too heavy; the robber hadn't had such beefy shoulders. The second looked mean and defiant, but his face was all wrong, too angular and shifty-looking.

Number three made her pause. In many ways he matched her memory of the robber. His complexion was even worse than she'd noticed the day of the robbery, but acne sometimes got worse under stress. His weight and height seemed right, but something was wrong. She moved her gaze to the last man, rejecting him because his jaw was too broad and his face didn't strike her as familiar.

"It could be the third from the left," Matt said slowly.

"Take a good look," the detective cautioned.

The line of men turned, giving a view of profiles with bumpy and smooth noses, jutting and small chins. Again Jennie easily eliminated three, but the one Matt had mentioned left her puzzled. He did look very much like the thief, but she wasn't positive one way or the other.

"Yes, he's familiar," Matt said, again indicating the man she'd dubbed Number Three.

"Ms. Martin," the detective asked, "do you recognize any of these men?"

"I'm not sure."

"Take your time," he said patiently.

She did take time, so much that the two men in the room with her shifted positions a bit restlessly.

"It definitely isn't the first or the second," she said, glad to be positive about that. "Nor the fourth."

"What about the third man from the left?" Woodbury moved to the opposite side of the room.

"This is even more difficult than I expected," she said, fully aware of how serious her accusation could be.

"We want you to be sure," the detective said. "Guesses won't stand up in court."

The men standing on the other side of the window were all so young, she wondered how many were actual suspects. Did the police use anyone available to stand in at a lineup? Maybe some of the men were in jail for other reasons; one or more could be policemen deliberately trying to look tough.

Still hesitating she found the silence in the room oppressive. The detective and Matt wanted her to make a decision; she could sense their restlessness even though they said nothing.

"I can't be sure," she said at last. "Number Three is the only possibility, but I can't say I definitely recognize him."

"You don't recognize him, then?" Woodbury asked.

"I'm just not sure."

She wanted to agree with Matt's identification but couldn't. Nor could she positively assert that he was wrong. Something about the suspect didn't seem right, but she didn't know what it was.

"Mr. Nichols?" the policeman asked.

"I'd say that's him," Matt said, his confident statement bothering Jennie even more. "Everything about him fits."

She didn't want a vicious thief to go free; the easy thing to do would be agree with the other witness. Matt was taller and could have gotten a better look at the man. At best the doubled glass of the inner and outer windows of the jewelry store was distorting. She'd actually seen his face only a moment before he'd donned the mask. His shabby jacket had attracted her attention; here, all the men being viewed wore T-shirts or sport shirts.

Admitting to herself she could be wrong didn't change her mind about not pointing him out as the thief.

Impatient with her own indecisiveness Jennie felt as though she'd somehow failed. As soon as the ordeal was over, she practically raced toward the exit.

"Jennie, wait!" Matt caught up with her in a few easy strides, the soles of his wingtip shoes loud on the old terrazzo floor.

"I couldn't be sure," she said.

"You have to be careful about it," he said, smiling his understanding.

"He could go to jail for a long time."

"If he's guilty," Matt said.

"You identified him."

"I think he's the man I saw. I had to say so."

"Yes."

"It doesn't matter whether you agree with me. The case isn't closed yet."

"I just want to be sure."

"Look, I have an appointment." He glanced at his watch. "But I think we should talk about this. Until the police find the stolen jewelry, all they have is us. That sort of makes us a team."

"I guess it does." She smiled at his reasoning.

"We should have a meeting to compare notes. Maybe you noticed something I didn't."

"Or it could be the other way around." It would relieve her mind to know exactly what he was thinking.

"When are you through today?" he asked.

"Five."

"Um, it will be closer to six before I can get away. Look,

36

we have to eat anyway. Let me pick you up and we'll talk while we have dinner."

He was going out of his way to make it sound like something besides a date, but she wasn't sure.

"If I am wrong, you'd be doing me and the suspect a favor," he persisted.

"I don't have anything to add to what I said."

"I always do," he said with a grin. "Is six-thirty all right?"

"Yes." She sighed to herself, not at all sure it was a good idea.

"Fine. See you then!"

He hurried off, leaving her a little stunned. She'd agreed to have dinner with him, but she still had compelling reasons to refuse.

The afternoon went too fast. Jennie liked her job, most of which involved studying medical reports and making recommendations to pay or not pay claims, but it wasn't exciting enough to make time fly. Today, uneasiness about seeing Matt made her want to put off the close of the work day.

There was time to change outfits after the bus dropped her a block from her apartment, but she didn't. Even switching to something as casual as slacks and a sweater would mean she'd made special preparations for the dinner with Matt; it was important not to think of it as a date. She was only going with him because identifying a possible thief was very serious. For her own peace of mind she had to be sure.

He came to her door still wearing a business suit, but the tie was gone and his shirt was partially unbuttoned. Fine, dark hairs curled in the exposed V below the strong column of his throat, and he moved into her living room with the athletic grace of a man who had developed his whole body sensibly and evenly instead of concentrating on a special set of muscles for a single competitive activity.

"I've thought about that man all afternoon," she said as they walked to his car. "It's so hard to be sure after just a glimpse through the window."

"It is," he agreed, "but let's have something to eat before we talk. I didn't have time for lunch."

"Neither did I." She didn't explain that her supervisor had urged her to take extra time but the grim mission at the police station had killed her interest in lunch.

"Do you like Chinese food?"

"Love it."

The Mandarin Gate was a one-story modern brick building, but everything possible had been done to make the interior seem like a Chinese fantasy land. Carved teak screens were scattered at random to give the close-packed little tables an illusion of privacy, and the red silk brocade on the walls served as a backdrop for paintings and carvings. Every five feet or so an elaborately decorated lantern hung from the ceiling, each one different with Oriental scenes illuminated by low-watt bulbs inside the paper globes. Their table was a square about the size of a checkerboard covered with a starched white cloth, and the water glasses were a thick ruby red.

"Would you like to order one entrée or try the dinner for two?" Matt asked.

"I enjoy trying new foods."

"Good. Let's see. On the dinner for two we get cashew chicken, sweet and sour pork, and pepper steak. They don't mind substitutes, if you'd like to try some other dish."

"No, they sound fine."

The young Chinese waiter in a red cotton jacket seemed to know only a few phrases of English, but Matt ordered patiently, repeating everything slowly and pointing to the menu to get across the idea of extra egg rolls.

He really was a terribly likable person, Jennie thought.

It would be nice having him for a friend, if a single man and woman could be just friends.

By the time they finished the wonton soup, she knew he had a university degree and an M.A. in business, but he seemed genuinely interested in her two-year community college degree and her job. They talked about family, skirting the subject of her husband's death. He spoke affectionately of his brother Jon, who was going to marry a woman named Sibella. She was a fashion consultant and gave color readings.

"I've been curious about them," Jennie said, "but haven't wanted to spend money to have one."

"Sibella gave me a reading as a Christmas present. According to her I should wear white suits in the summer and anything chocolate colored. Can you imagine my drycleaning bill in July?"

"Maybe it's better to rely on what you like. Blondes should wear pastels, I guess, but I love red and navy and vivid fall colors."

"Don't even consider changing! You're a dynamite lady just the way you are."

Her cheeks felt warm, and she was mad at herself for blushing like a naive schoolgirl. She wasn't used to compliments from an attractive man, especially one who sounded so sincere.

They laughed when he surprised his tastebuds with an overdose of hot mustard sauce and when she tried with little success to manipulate wooden chopsticks. He was amusing, telling her about his passion for racket sports and chili dogs; he was amused, hearing her tell about growing up in a town where they showed movies on the side of a building on Saturday nights in the summer. The table was so small it wasn't surprising they bumped knees more than once.

They'd come to talk about identifying the robbery suspect, but neither mentioned it until after they broke open fortune cookies and laughed at the ambiguous predictions.

"You will find the answer to your problem," she read.

"That's better than *Someone near and dear has a surprise for you.* It doesn't say whether it will be a pleasant one."

"I hope it will be."

He smiled broadly. "We haven't said anything about your problem yet. You know, Jennie, you can't let this witness business get you down."

"No, I guess not. I just want to be very sure before I say anything."

"That's what you should do. I could be wrong, but I have to say what I think too. You should do the same."

"That one man certainly looked a lot like the thief."

"If he is, the police will find more evidence. Don't let it bother you, if you can't agree with me."

As though to demonstrate there was more to spring than sunshine and budding, a sudden rain squall caught them without coats or umbrellas as they were leaving the restaurant. Matt insisted she wait inside the door while he ran for the car, but she still got damp taking a few steps to the car door. His jacket was wet, more chocolate- than sand-colored now, and she teased that his sister-in-law-to-be would approve of his damp look.

"We've had fun, even if we didn't solve the problem of the robbery suspect," he said, stopping beside her building.

"Yes. I'm sorry I'm not sure about the man you identified."

"Don't be. They shouldn't have had us in there together, but sometimes small-town police-work is sloppy."

"I wouldn't call Burdick a small town." Laughter had come easily all evening, but hers was strained now. It was time to go inside, but she wasn't eager to leave him.

"You must be cold," he said, touching her leg where

rain spots were only beginning to dry on the skirt of her dress.

"Yes, I should go in. Thank you for dinner."

"Thank you for your company. Bachelor dining isn't the kick my married friends think it is."

"Do you eat out every night?"

"No. More often than not I end up throwing something frozen in the microwave."

He didn't fit her image of the lonely bachelor, not Matt with his easy sense of humor and appealing openness.

"We really should do this again," he said solemnly. "And not so I can try to change your mind about what you did or didn't see."

"I don't think so," she said, forcing out the words with some difficulty.

"Let's just leave our options open," he said, sliding closer and separating her hands, locked together on her lap.

She intended to dash to her door through the diminishing rain, but he brought her fingers to his lips, planting a soft kiss on her knuckles. The delicate veins in her wrist pulsated with a strong beat, but her brain sounded a warning: men like Matt could be extremely hazardous to the heart.

Intent on leaving, Jennie fumbled for the door handle in the dark, but his hand slid to the back of her neck, his long, cool fingers caressing her throat.

"Jennie."

The door swung open as she turned to protest, her lips colliding with his warm, seeking ones. His light kiss had a special gentleness, lasting only moments, but the impact was as surprising as it was sensual.

"Don't say anything!" he warned severely. "I know when lips are ready to be kissed."

Feeling that she should scold him, she fled from the car

instead, running through puddles on the walk that splashed up and soaked her feet.

Later, warmed by a shower and a cup of spearmint tea, she was still thinking about Matt as she got ready to go to sleep. Going to dinner had been against her better judgment, but she did have fun. His kiss had done nothing to spoil the pleasant evening, but it was interfering with her peace of mind.

Lying in bed, listening to soft music on the radio in hopes of becoming drowsy, she wondered if it was time to stop depriving herself of male companionship. Jennie had a hard time remembering how it felt to be in love with Kirk; it seemed as if pain and guilt blocked out all the good memories. The sound of a deep voice, the touch of a comforting hand on hers, and the companionship of a kind man were pleasures she'd long denied herself. Would it be so terrible to have a person like Matt as a friend?

Dejected, feeling her loneliness more acutely than she had in a long time, she reached over and turned off the radio. Jennie drew up her knees and elbows and cuddled against the pillow, very much afraid it was a mistake to want more from life than she had now.

CHAPTER THREE

Backs! Jennie closed the folder and stretched, sure that back-injury claims were the trickiest and most troublesome she had to handle. Her instincts told her here was another case that should be paid by workmen's compensation instead of her company, but it would take more information to be sure. Some days she felt like Sherlock Holmes, sifting through medical jargon and clients' claims to find the real culprit, which often turned out to be an irresponsible employer or a careless claimant.

One of the last to leave the office for the evening, she had to rush to catch her bus. It was already in sight as she hurried from the building, so she didn't bother to open her umbrella. The off-and-on rainfall was only a light drizzle now, and she was beginning to long for a sunny day.

The case on her desk still bothered her as she moved to the rear of the bus without finding a seat. Certainly the doctors had ordered enough tests. They were practically test-happy these days, and she couldn't blame them, not with the threat of lawsuits becoming a major professional problem. First thing in the morning she'd mail a request for additional information to the claimant. Until she checked for discrepancies between that and his emergency-room statement, the case would be on hold.

More things than a back case were on hold in her life right now. Decisions were relatively easy to make in her job, because she had all the documentation necessary. Remembering a face seen for only a few seconds before a traumatic robbery was entirely different. She could add a bit of spice to her job by thinking of herself as an insurance detective, but there was nothing intriguing about being a witness to a real crime. A man's freedom was at stake; if she made a mistake, an innocent person could be sent to jail or a dangerous, guilty one could be set free to commit more crimes. The next time he might be jittery enough to shoot someone. She fervently wished she could feel more certain about recognizing the suspect in the lineup like Matt did.

Certainty. She said the word to herself, remembering what her grandfather used to say: "The only sure things are death and taxes." Before meeting Matt, she'd been pretty certain about the course of her life. There was nothing adventurous about the way she spent her days, but her life had many small pleasures; she liked her job, her friends, hobbies like gardening and sewing. It was a low-risk life-style, with no big highs and no chance of failing anyone but herself.

The bus stopped with a lurch, and she had to squeeze past a stout man who apparently was too lost in thought to notice he was blocking the aisle. Jennie missed the chance to get off at her stop, but she got off at the next and started walking back, skirting puddles under a gray sky.

After collecting the mail from her box set into the wall of the walkway that led to the parking lot in the back, she started down her stairs, opening the door and jumping when something brushed against her foot. A long parcel wrapped in florist's tissue had been propped between the doors and had fallen when she opened the outer one.

Excited in spite of her determination not to be, she went inside and carefully peeled away the paper to reveal a single vivid red rose, the velvety bud making her forget she'd ever been cynical about cut flowers.

The card read: *Don't let anyone talk you into pink.*

There was no name, but she remembered telling Matt she preferred vivid colors, not the pastels that were supposed to look good on blondes. More pleased than she wanted to admit, she took the bloom from its bed of ferns and touched it against the tip of her nose, inhaling its lovely scent.

Later, catching up on correspondence to her parents, brother, and friends back in Hopewell, she more than half expected Matt to call. She didn't know whether to be relieved or disappointed when the phone was silent all evening.

She did get a call at her office the next day, another summons to police headquarters. At least it was a warm, sunny day. She compensated for her lost lunch by enjoying the walk to the station.

Detective Woodbury was in his office waiting for her. There was no sign of Matt, but she wouldn't admit to herself she was disappointed. Maybe it wasn't good police procedure to have both witnesses come at the same time, as Matt had said.

"Have you found any of the jewelry?" she asked, wishing the police would catch the thief with the stolen merchandise so this whole thing could be done with.

"Not yet. What we need is for you to take a look at two men. Do exactly what you did last time, just tell me what you think."

"Are they both under arrest?"

Staring at strangers was so awkward, even if they couldn't see through their side of the special glass. She wondered if they had families, girlfriends, maybe wives. Were they employed? How did they spend their time?

"Let's take a look," the detective said, avoiding her question.

He led her to the same room, but this time another man joined them, a Mr. Simons from the prosecutor's office. He asked her several questions, none of them new, then told her to look at the two men.

One of them was the suspect Matt had identified so positively. This time he did seem familiar, but she realized it was only because he'd been in the first lineup. The other man was a little taller and surly-looking, with small, mean eyes. He certainly looked like a criminal, but he definitely wasn't the jewel thief.

"It's not the new man," she said immediately. "I'm still not sure about the one Mr. Nichols identified."

"You do remember him from the other time?" Detective Woodbury didn't sound very happy.

"Yes. He looks a lot like the thief, with his brown hair and poor complexion. His height and weight are about right, but I just don't know. Maybe I was so scared, my brain erased his face. Is that possible?" Instead of being more positive one way or the other, she was more confused.

"Anything's possible." The detective sounded weary.

"I'd really like to help."

"It won't help us in court if you aren't sure of yourself," Mr. Simons said.

"I'm sorry, but I'm not." She was regretful but not apologetic. Nothing would be worse than to identify the wrong person. She could tell both men were disappointed in her, perhaps writing her off as a silly woman who didn't know what she'd seen. She'd have to live with their opinion even if they were scornful. As much as she wanted to identify him as the thief, she couldn't.

"Can you say for certain this isn't the man you saw putting on a ski mask in front of Garber's jewelry store?" the assistant prosecutor asked.

"No, but—"

"I think that will be enough," he said to Woodbury. "You can go, Ms. Martin. Thank you for your cooperation."

She walked thoughtfully toward the exit, wondering if the damp, rather sour smell in the corridor was the scent of human misery. It certainly made her unhappy to be in this building, and she wasn't being accused of anything, unless it was being a careless witness.

"We've got to stop meeting like this!"

"Matt!"

He came toward her, his smile making her forget she was anywhere near the jail.

"You've had a look at some new suspects? No, don't tell me. At least they're doing it professionally this time."

"There's a man here from the prosecutor's office—a Mr. Simons."

"They must think they have a case."

"I got your rose. It was lovely. Thank you."

"You knew it was from me." He sounded pleased.

"Yes. Well, I have to get back to work."

"No time for lunch? I shouldn't be long."

"No, my desk is swamped."

"Wait, don't leave so quickly. Are you free Saturday?"

"I don't know," she fibbed, still hesitant about beginning something that might become too important.

"I'll call you tonight." He started to dash away.

"Matt, I don't—"

"You'll want to hear if I finger anybody, kid," he said in an awful imitation of Humphrey Bogart that made her smile.

That evening she was ready to hop off at her bus stop, eager to get home even though his call might not come for hours. At least she knew what her answer would be. Avoiding all men had meant cutting herself off from nearly half of the interesting people in the world. Just because she had dinner with Matt didn't mean she was on the threshold of a great romance. More than likely, he had scads of single women at his beck and call. A few dates would mean little to him, and when he found out their friendsh had to be platonic, that would be the end of it.

He didn't disappoint her. The phone was ringing as sh opened the door.

"Did you just get home?" he asked.

"Yes."

"I'm still at the office, then I have to take a client dinner. I was afraid you'd be asleep before I got rid him."

"I usually stay up for the eleven o'clock news."

"So do I. Maybe I should get cable. Watch the nev earlier and go to bed earlier, but I'm a night person."

"So am I," she admitted. "It takes me hours to get goir in the morning."

She immediately regretted having told him that. H might think she was a poor witness because the robber had taken place early in the day.

"I can't imagine you not being at your best anytime."

Remember, he flirts with waitresses, she warned hersel not wanting to believe his sweet talk was entirely sincer

"Did you see the two suspects?" she asked, wanting change the subject.

"Yes." He hesitated, then added, "I still think he's tl one."

"The same man?"

"Yes. His name is Neil Blockman."

She wasn't glad to know that. Being able to think of hir by name made the burden of her indecisiveness eve heavier.

"Who was the other one?"

"Someone they arrested trying to rob a fast-food plac It was a long shot, but since they had him for one crim they thought we might as well take a look."

"Has the thief—the suspect—been arrested?"

"Blockman?"

"Yes."

"I think the man from the prosecutor's office was there to make that decision," he explained.

"Oh." She hadn't given him any reason not to file charges, not when they had one positive witness.

"About Saturday night," he began.

She was glad to talk about something besides being a witness.

"I have community theater tickets. It's the last play of the season. Would you like to go?"

"Yes, that would be fun."

"Dinner first? I'll pick you up a little before six."

"I'll look forward to it." She would, in spite of some nagging reservations.

The dress she was making for Martha's retirement party could be finished by Saturday evening if she really worked, she thought after they hung up. Walking into her sewing room with its convenient clutter, she looked at the elegant raspberry silk-blend, an expensive remnant she'd purchased at a sale. Because the fabric was so dressy for her usual needs, she'd chosen a simple pattern, scoop-necked and sleeveless with an elasticized waist and a narrow fabric sash. The garment was assembled, but she had the touchy job of putting in a long back zipper. If it wasn't done perfectly on the first try, the stitch marks would show from ripping it out. Should she make this date with Matt more important by finishing the dress? She'd leave it to fate, she decided. If she could install the zipper so it looked perfect, then she'd hurry to do the finishing work before Saturday evening.

More enthused than she'd been in a long time about sewing something for herself, Jennie made a quick tuna sandwich for dinner and got to work.

She pinned the zipper, then decided such fine material demanded basting, taking the time to hand-stitch it loosely before sewing it on the machine. The result was a professionally neat job, the closure installed without a single tuck or pull. Jennie was so pleased she immediately started putting the facings on the neckline and armholes.

Her parents called long distance for one of their frequent chats. Jennie exchanged news with her mother and father, omitting any mention of Matt, although she did tell them the latest developments on the robbery. Then Tonya rang and talked for a bit, and Jennie went back to her sewing, not even bothering to look at a clock.

The third call of the evening prompted her to check the time on her way to answer it. The clock on the stove said it was after eleven.

"Am I interrupting your news?"

"Matt?"

"I just got home. You were still up, weren't you?"

"Yes, I didn't realize it was after eleven."

"Let me tell you my version of the nightly news."

"All right."

"Flash: it's still possible for a jaded bachelor to meet a lovely lady in a dreary little town in the Midwest."

"Burdick isn't dreary!" She was flushing with pleasure, forgetting to remind herself that he did like to flirt.

"I don't think so, but I just spent the evening with a New Yorker. He wasn't impressed by the night life in our humble village."

"You're exaggerating."

"Not about finding a lovely lady."

"Have you been drinking?"

"Suspicious lady! One rusty nail after dinner. Something else is making me a little giddy. You wouldn't like to go out for pizza, would you?"

"Now? No, thanks."

"Night life in our town is pretty limited. That was the best I could come up with to lure you out into the evening."

"You're teasing!"

"No, it's the Welsh in me. My mother's grandmother,

no, my grandmother's mother, came from a place you need thirty-two letters to spell. Near Llandudno, and try pronouncing that when you're not absolutely sober!"

"It's your great-grandmother, either way you say it!" she said, catching on to his joke.

"Well, either way, she had to be a great speller. Or else she left because she was a lousy speller."

He was being silly to make her laugh, and he succeeded, joining in enthusiastically.

"I knew your laugh would sound wonderful over the phone. Next time I'm going to record it and play it to my clients when General Motors drops five points."

"Good night, Matt."

"Good night, sweet Jennie." Suddenly his voice was a husky caress that made her shiver with a new kind of intensity. "I'll be out of town tomorrow, but I'll see you soon."

"Saturday," she said, knowing he didn't need reminding.

Hugging her arms across her chest, she wondered about his frivolous but sweet call. She turned out the light in the sewing room and started to get ready for bed, hoping her dress would live up to its promise, hoping even more that Saturday wouldn't be a big disappointment.

Saturday brought more rain, a dreary drizzle that showed no sign of stopping as Jennie dressed for dinner and the theater. She laid out her raincoat, regretting the necessity of wearing it over what had turned out to be one of the nicest dresses she'd ever made. The raspberry silk bodice hugged her breasts and tapered to a perfect fit, emphasizing her slender waist. She was glad it was ready for tonight, telling herself it would save a big rush to finish it for Martha's party.

He rang the buzzer, smiling when she opened the door. "You look beautiful," he said with such soft-spoken sincerity, she didn't think of dismissing his compliment as simple flirting.

"Thank you."

His raincoat was open, revealing a midnight-blue pinstripe suit.

"You didn't follow your color chart," she teased, sure that no pat advice could make him look more appealing.

"I can go home and change."

"No, don't do that! You look very handsome."

He laughed, telling her without words she shouldn't take him—or herself—so seriously.

He took her to a little restaurant tucked between a hotel and the tallest bank building in town. The Golden Fleece was no larger than an average-size living room, but clever planning had managed to divide it into semiprivate little niches using high-backed booth and seats.

"Nick, how are you?" Matt said to a heavyset but handsome man with thick blue-black hair who met them just inside the door.

"Couldn't be better! You're gonna be a best man pretty soon, I hear."

"If Jon has his way."

"That's great! Your table," he said, leading them to a corner booth for two. "The rack of lamb is the best we've had in a long time, but we're nearly out. If you're interested, I'll have the chef hold it. For fish we have orange ruffie; that's scalloped. You should try the tiny potatoes with parsley and butter. We took the sirloin tips off the menu; my supplier wasn't doing what he should have for us." He helped Jennie with her raincoat while he talked, then waited until Matt removed his and disappeared with both coats.

"That was the talking menu," Matt said. "There isn't a printed one. You can order any kind of steak there is, then tell the waiter what you want with it."

"Do you come here often?"

"Always for special occasions. You can't get in without a reservation, and if Nick doesn't like someone, that person will never get a table."

"You have to be a friend of his to eat here?"

"His customers are all friends. He could serve ten times this number every evening, but he likes a personal touch."

"It sounds like you do too."

"Tonight I do."

They both had the rack of lamb, served with buttered potatoes, carrots, and asparagus, followed by cups of aromatic black coffee.

Matt signed the check, not even taking out a credit card. If he was trying to impress her, he'd succeeded, but not because he frequented a restaurant with no price list. Rather, his friendliness put her at ease, proving that dinner alone with an attractive man didn't have to be a cause for anxiety. Even without knowing how long it had been since she'd had anything remotely resembling a date, he made it seem natural and right to be there with him.

His season tickets for the Burdick Community Theater were in the fifth row center, and he seemed to know most of the people sitting around them, introducing Jennie to more friends than she could possibly remember. She was beginning to see how the town could seem small to someone who'd always lived there, but she'd never met people who were more poised and congenial.

The houselights darkened and those on the stage went on to reveal the set, a meeting house in colonial Salem. The play, *The Crucible,* was about witchcraft and adolescent psychology and was more thought provoking than entertaining; but Jennie became engrossed. Matt's arm lay against her bare one on the double armrests of the theater seats, and the drama on the stage was only beginning when he reached down and took her hand in his.

In the play the motive of the young girls who accused other villagers of witchcraft became more and more suspect, but Jennie was too distracted by Matt's hand to relate the play to her own anxieties about being a witness. His fingers were long and strong, caressing her wrist and exploring the creases in her palm with tingling gentleness. When she made a ball of her fist, intending to discourage him, he only covered it with his whole hand, stroking her knuckles and the curl of her fingers.

There was one intermission, with tiny cups of coffee served in the green room. Matt didn't join any of the groups of people who called out or waved to him, seeming to prefer her company alone.

"Did I mention you look stunning tonight?" he asked, smiling down at her as though they were the only people in the crowded room.

She tried to ignore the warm rush of blood to her cheeks by switching the conversation to the play.

"Do you think the girls are faking?" she asked.

"Maybe a little. Or maybe it was mass hysteria. Historians are still debating about the real Salem witch trials, I guess."

"Maybe they wanted the attention."

"My theory is there was a lot of unhealthy sexual repression in those days," he said with a teasing smile.

The lights blinked.

"Time to go back to our seats," she said, moving toward the door without commenting on his theory.

This time he didn't wait until the lights went out to capture her hand and hold it against the side of his thigh. In the moment of blackness before the stage was illuminated, he brought it to his lips and lightly kissed the top. Jennie tried to wiggle free, but he had very persuasive fingers.

The rain had stopped by the time they left the theater, leaving the fragrance of damp earth and budding bushes in the air. Putting his arm on her shoulders he walked so close his thigh brushed against her hip. She wasn't used to the kind of intimacy he seemed to take for granted, but she didn't want to make an issue of it, so she said nothing.

"Would you like a drink?" he asked when they were back in his car."

"No, thank you, but I really did enjoy the play."

"I'm glad."

He started the car without looking at her. She stayed near the door, leaving a wide gap between them on the seat, content with a silence that seemed natural. Had she only imagined the magic in his touch? Maybe it was the setting, the drama onstage and the coziness of the darkened theater, that had made the evening seem enchanted.

Instead of stopping by the front curb he drove to the parking area in back of her building, cutting the motor and turning off the lights. She started to tell him again how much she'd enjoyed dinner and the play, but he didn't give her a chance.

If he'd said anything, even a single word, she would have come to her senses and said a hasty good-night. Instead he turned sideways, moving closer as he did, and traced the outline of her lips with the tip of one finger, creating shock waves of sensation. When he leaned toward her and pressed a soft kiss on the corner of her mouth, Jennie's resistance melted like butter on hot iron, leaving her a little giddy and more than a little shaken.

Then she did remember to say, "Thank you for the nice evening."

"The nicest part is just beginning," he said seductively, caressing the back of her neck with one hand and letting the other rest on her nylon-clad knee as he slowly repeated his kiss.

His lips were firm and smooth, moving over hers with practiced effectiveness but with a special sweetness that made his kisses different from any she'd experienced before. He enjoyed kissing her, she realized. That was the secret of the pleasure she felt. They weren't just a prelude to put her in the mood for lovemaking.

"You taste wonderful," he said softly, then kissed her more deeply.

"I have to go in," she said urgently, pulling away and knowing she should have done so sooner.

"I'm sorry." He moved away. "Don't go, Jennie. I won't do anything you don't want me to."

"I'm too old to do this in a car." She didn't like the way her words sounded, but it was too late to take them back.

"I'll see you to the door."

"No, really, it's only a few steps."

"I don't like your entryway," he said seriously. "Someone could hide at the bottom of the steps and you wouldn't notice until it was too late."

He followed her to the sunken stairwell, where her front door seemed invitingly close, illuminated by a yellow bulb in the fixture over it.

"I left a light on," she said, feeling a need to point out there wasn't any danger. "Thank you, Matt. The dinner was very nice. So was the play."

He followed silently as she went to her door and fumbled in her small beaded handbag for the key. When he took it and opened the door, her face revealed her uneasiness.

"I'm not coming in, not tonight." His smile was tender and understanding. "Good night, Jennie."

He hurried up the steps and didn't look back.

After hanging her coat in the closet she went directly to the bedroom, catching a glimpse of herself in the big mirror above the dresser. A breeze had stirred her usually sleek blond cap, but more than this made her image almost unfamiliar. There was a dreamy look in her eyes that was totally foreign to her face, as well as new rosiness in her cheeks. Her lips were bright pink, still tingling from the tantalizing contact of his lips, and part of her wished him back. Her body was young and healthy, and tonight had been a vivid contrast to her long, self-imposed loneliness. Feelings she'd thought dead were clamoring at her senses, confusing and disturbing her.

Matt was handsome, sexy in a wholesome, appealing way. And he was interested in her. Being alone so much at the end of her marriage and afterward hadn't made her insensitive to the spark of desire in a man's eyes.

Removing her dress and draping it over a padded hanger, she was lost in thought, startled when the phone interrupted her daydreaming.

"I wanted to say good-night," Matt said.

"You're home already?" Glancing at the clock she realized nearly fifteen minutes had passed while she thought about the evening.

"My house is on Warren Street. It's not far."

He told her about the big Victorian home he'd renovated, living on the ground level and renting two apartments on the second floor and one on the third.

"I should have driven you past it," he said. "Next time I will."

Next time? He seemed certain that there would be another time, but Jennie wasn't sure. Matt was a terrific person; he deserved someone special. Once she had felt the same way about Kirk, but she'd failed him. Their marriage started to go bad almost from the beginning, and the more she pleaded with him to spend time with her instead of racing around the countryside, the worse his obsession grew. She didn't question his love for her, but when she tried to return it, she was inadequate, not understanding him and perhaps not trying hard enough.

She was still the same person; conservative and unadventurous Kirk had often called her.

"Thank you again for the evening," she said to Matt.

"It was my pleasure. I want to see you again, Jennie.

Soon. Tomorrow I have to go to Detroit to deliver the ring for my brother. Would you like to ride along?"

"I'm sorry. I can't." She wasn't a good liar; her refusal sounded stiff and unconvincing.

He didn't seem to notice. "I'll call you later, then. Good night, Jennie."

"Good night."

"Oh, don't hang up. I almost forgot to tell you, red is definitely your color. You were beautiful in that dress."

"Thank you." She wanted to say more, to let him know she was grateful for his kindness and attentiveness, but she couldn't. Anything she might say would sound like goodbye. Her better judgment insisted it was best if they never met again, but her heart was a rebel. Another day she'd have to end their friendship; tonight she wanted to fall asleep thinking of how nice he was.

Slipping into her faded pink flannel gown she reluctantly decided that avoiding emotional entanglements was still the wisest course. She wasn't ready to become close to another man. Maybe someday, in the far future, she'd marry again, but it wouldn't be fair to encourage Matt now. Inside she was withered and empty, like a garden abandoned to weeds and thistles. For a short time she'd wanted him very much in the way a woman craves a man, but sex was only a snare if she couldn't be the kind of woman he deserved. If he became serious, she might hurt him. If he didn't, she'd be taking a big risk at a time when she wasn't strong enough for more pain and rejection.

Her sleep was troubled, and she awoke early the next morning, too restless to stay in bed. Like Cinderella at the ball she'd had a magical evening, but a glass slipper wasn't going to change her life. Matt might be right for her, but his timing was all wrong. A part of her had died with Kirk, and resurrecting it was going to be a long, lonely struggle. She couldn't expect anyone to share it. Refusing Matt now was easier than waiting to see what developed.

Maybe, she thought, intending to console herself but failing miserably, Matt wasn't all that interested anyway.

CHAPTER FOUR

Monday morning Jennie stared at the file on the back case, intending to send a routine form letter asking for more information, but her mind kept bouncing around, more often veering toward Matt than her work. It wasn't like her to lose concentration!

After forcing herself to type an address on the envelope, she put it aside and reviewed the basics of the case, checking the appropriate boxes on the request form and signing her name and office extension. Sealing the envelope and putting it in the basket for outgoing mail seemed like a major accomplishment: two minutes spent without thinking about Matt.

Even without her other reservations she'd be wary of such a quick and overwhelming attraction. Was loneliness causing her to imagine a wild infatuation, one that would wane as quickly as it had flared up? Impetuous romance was for teenagers, not a responsible woman who was still recovering from a failed marriage that ended tragically.

By the end of the day she'd built an impressive case against seeing Matt again. Weighed against the potential for hurting both of them, refusing to see him was the only sensible thing to do. They'd forget each other in a short time with no harm done. It went against all her principles to use him as a crutch for her loneliness.

Unfortunately he didn't call that evening. Jennie was ready with a carefully rehearsed speech and enough logical arguments to sway the Supreme Court. Instead his next call came at her office the following day, just as she was leaving for the noon break.

"Meet me for lunch," he suggested.

She imagined trying to explain how she felt in a crowded restaurant with both of them hurrying to get back to work on time.

"No, I'm afraid I can't."

He accepted her refusal without question, knowing when he called she might not be able to get away on a moment's notice.

"After work, then. I'll come by around six-thirty and we can have dinner."

Again she envisioned a busy dining place where they were likely to see people he knew. Going out with him again would only make telling him more difficult.

"Matt, I don't think we should go out." She spoke very softly, even though the partitions on three sides of her cubbyhole muffled her conversations.

"Not at all?" He sounded more surprised than angry.

"I didn't plan to tell you like this. There are good reasons; you'll have to believe that. It's not that I don't like you, because I do, very much." Her prepared speech came out in a rush of words. "This is just the wrong time for me. I hope you'll understand."

"I don't," he said flatly.

"I can't explain on the phone."

"Then meet me somewhere." He sounded upset. "You name the time and place."

"There isn't any point—nothing will change."

"You're saying so long, just like that, and not even talking it over?" He sounded like a man trying hard not to lose his temper. "I thought you had a good time Saturday."

"I did—that's part of the trouble. Please, Matt, it's just not the right time. I am sorry." Her throat was tight, and she wanted the conversation to end before she embarrassed herself by crying.

"So am I," he said harshly.

"Good-bye."

She dropped the receiver in place and picked up the papers on the next case demanding her attention. They could have been Chinese for all the sense she made of the little black squiggles on the pages. The rest of the day was much the same, and Jennie went home with a heavy heart.

She couldn't wander into a relationship with her eyes shut and her heart exposed. The healing process had been slow and painful after Kirk's death, and always the shadow of guilt lingered in the back of her mind. Knowing he was headed for serious trouble, she'd kept quiet, making excuses to his family and hers, pretending things would be better in the future. Even when she thought of leaving him, hoping the shock would jolt him into a more sane lifestyle, she had said nothing to others. Somehow, she should have forced him to get help, and both had needed counseling about their life together. Instead her ineffective pleas had driven a wedge between them until they were strangers sharing little more than living space.

Coming to Burdick had been an escape. When a friend from high school invited her to share an apartment, she'd left the farm, her family and his, hoping to get away from constant reminders of Kirk and their marriage. In a sense she'd succeeded. Her pain had lessened and her heart became numb. Now, by her beginning to care for another man, all the old doubts flared up again. She wasn't ready for romance and didn't want to risk becoming close.

Feeling restless and at loose ends Jennie decided to clean out the sewing room, where sorting remnants and scrap materials from old projects would keep her busy. After dinner she turned the radio to her favorite FM music station and began weeding out useless leftovers. The pile of small usable pieces grew to a sizable mound, and she decided to begin a new project: doll clothes for her nieces. Her worn fur-lined gloves would make stunning little capes, and short scraps of trim couldn't be put to a better use. Next payday she'd buy new dolls for both girls and make fabulous wardrobes as Christmas presents.

Though she'd come up with a way to occupy her time, filling the void in her heart was an entirely different problem. Every word of her phone conversation with Matt went through her mind again and again with more regret than satisfaction. He liked her; he'd never hinted at love. Wasn't she assuming a lot, worrying about the consequences of a relationship that might never be more than a casual friendship?

A friend from the office called, wanting to know if Jennie needed a ride to a baby shower later in the week. She didn't, because Tonya was picking her up, but suggested the three of them could go together. A few minutes later a woman who'd been in a water aerobics class with her the previous year phoned, wanting Jennie to help publicize a Red Cross water safety program. She said yes, glad to give up a few hours of spare time for a good cause, even if it meant manning a table at the shopping mall on some future Saturday.

She went back to work, trying to decide whether she'd ever use the strips of used cloth set aside to make a braided seat for the Boston rocker in her bedroom, when the door buzzer sounded. Her phone rang frequently, but she wasn't used to nighttime visitors who came without calling first.

Matt stood on the other side of the storm door, looking much as he had when they first met. The collar of a faded plaid flannel shirt showed above the crew neck of a dark-green sweater, and the jeans clinging to his thighs were faded to a whitish-blue. A light rain had dampened his shoulders and left glistening drops on his windblown hair. He was frowning under the yellow light, silent until she opened the exterior door.

"Can I come in?"

Face to face with him she couldn't make herself say no

He stepped out of wet moccasins and left them on small rug beside the door.

"My shoes are wet," he said needlessly.

"I wonder if it will ever stop raining."

He wasn't there to comment on the weather. "We've go to talk, Jennie."

"Your hair is wet. I'll get you a towel."

He protested, but she hurried to the hall cupboard and took out one of her best fleecy rose bath-towels, handing to him, buying time to compose herself while he toweled his face and hair.

"About this 'wrong time' business," he said, walking t the kitchen and dropping the towel on the counter "—it' not enough to convince me."

He peeled off his sweater, draping it over a kitchen chai to dry, and went back to the living room, sitting down on the couch. She followed, standing uneasily on the othe side of the room. They were as wary as two people poise for battle, but neither showed any hostility.

"Jennie, your husband's dead, isn't he?"

"Yes! You know that!" Was he doubting her word? Sh was more puzzled than angry.

"How do you feel about it?"

"I regret it," she said carefully, not knowing what h expected.

"It happened a long time ago."

"Less than three years."

"What I need to know," he said with obvious difficulty "is whether you're still so much in love with him tha there's no room for anyone else in your life."

"How can I answer a question like that?" She walked t the window, looking up at the dark rectangle of glass.

"Honestly, I hope." He walked over to her, putting hi

hands on her shoulders. "I have to know if I'm competing with a ghost."

"Not competing, no." She turned to face him, seeing her own pain reflected in his dark eyes.

"Tell me what's standing in our way," he insisted.

"It's not that simple, Matt." Her hands were locked together and pressed against her midriff.

"I'm not going to walk away from you unless you convince me I should. Was your marriage a happy one?"

"No, not toward the end." This was the first time she'd admitted it to any other person. "Kirk was killed on a motorcycle. It was an obsession, racing around the countryside with his friends. I try to remember how he looked at our wedding or when we were dating in high school, but I always see him with a helmet, a black helmet."

"Are you still in love with him?"

Looking down to avoid his gaze she could hear the compassion in his voice and knew he hated asking. How could she make him understand what a total failure her marriage had become?

"Jennie?"

He stepped so close she could see his feet close to hers, his white crew socks only inches from her penny loafers.

Without looking up she said, "No, I'm not."

His deep sigh expressed so much relief, she looked at him and felt compelled to say more.

"His accident wasn't a surprise. I could see it coming. He was drinking too much, never staying home in the evening. Nothing I said or did made any difference. I should have been able to help him."

"You blame yourself for the accident?"

When she didn't answer, he put his arms around her, holding her close in a comforting hug.

"I understand." He held her for several moments.

Because she never talked about Kirk, confessing to Matt

made her feel very close to him, but it was an intimacy she resisted, slipping from his arms and backing away.

"About us . . ." Matt began.

"Nothing's changed," she said unhappily, still finding it hard to look directly into his eyes. "I'm not ready for any changes in my life right now."

"You mean you're not willing to take the risk of caring for someone?"

"I need more time."

"Jennie, I know it must be terrible losing your husband, but it happened. You can't change it, so you have to think of yourself."

"That doesn't mean—"

"It doesn't mean you should shut me out of your life."

"It isn't fair to you if—"

"I'll decide that."

"Will you let me finish a sentence?"

"No, I don't think so."

"Matt—"

"Jennie, if my sympathy helps, you can have carloads of it, but it's time to move on."

"That doesn't mean jumping into something rash."

"I'm thirty-two and I've never been married. Do you think I'm going to rush into a relationship just because you're beautiful and sweet and sexy?"

"You're making it so hard—"

"For you to get rid of me? I certainly hope so!" He touched her cheek with the backs of his fingers. "I don't know where we're headed," he said earnestly, "but I think we both deserve a chance to find out."

"I feel so empty. I don't think I'll be good for you."

"Give me a chance to find out. Give yourself a chance."

"Oh, Matt—"

"And don't 'Oh, Matt' me!"

He bent and kissed her, his lips caressing hers until she relaxed in the circle of his arms.

He wasn't quite as tall without shoes, and cuddling against his length brought a peaceful warmth, as though she'd momentarily surrendered her will to a benefactor.

Brushing aside a strand of hair from her cheek, he kissed it lightly, then massaged the hollows above her collarbone. The pads of his thumbs made her go limp.

"It's all right telling me," he said softly.

His other kisses had only been a prelude to the deep, bewitching way his mouth covered hers now, his special gentleness enhancing but not concealing the passion motivating him. For a fleeting moment the pressure on her lips was painfully intense, then her resistance melted, letting her enjoy the darting thrust of his tongue and the deep fullness of his kiss.

They separated awkwardly, as though both were surprised by the power of their kiss, and Jennie was defensive again, afraid because her body was so ready to respond. She felt an aching tightness like a steel hand gripping her, but she didn't want to be aroused this way. Her survival as a whole, sane person was based on self-control, denial, a deadening of her naturally sensual nature.

"You'd better go," she said.

"I will, but I'm not giving up."

She was embarrassed by the warm encouragement she'd given him, but several more tender kisses did much to wipe away her regret.

"When will I see you again?" He rested one hand on her waist, his eyes warning that only a definite promise would do.

"When do you want to?" She was stalling, trying to sort out her conflicting emotions.

"I'd rather not leave now."

One word would keep him there, but she was afraid even to imagine having him with her all night.

"Saturday," she said, grasping for a safe way to see him again. "I have to go to a retirement party for my supervisor. Remember? I was looking for her gift when the store was robbed. Would you like to come with me?"

"Yes, but I'd like to see you before then too."

"I need time to think, Matt."

"All right. When should I pick you up for the party?"

"Eight."

"Eight Saturday evening. It's not soon enough."

"Please . . ."

"Will it be easier for you if I don't call until then?"

"I think so."

"We'll go slow," he said with resignation. "I can be patient, as long as you don't shut me out."

He wasn't asking for promises, but her grateful smile gave him one. He collected his sweater and moccasins and left, not kissing her again.

Turning out the living room light she intended to go to bed, but instead sat on the edge of the couch wondering whether she was making a terrible mistake. The attraction between them was almost overwhelming, but she was scared, knowing how unprepared she was for any kind of relationship.

For the first time in many months Jennie opened a shallow cardboard storage box kept under her bed and took out the white leather album with her name and Kirk's embossed in gold on the cover. His older sister had given it to them as a wedding gift, and Jennie still kept it wrapped in blue tissue.

She turned to their formal wedding portrait, but not to study her husband's face sheepishly smiling into the camera and looking much too immature for the responsibilities of marriage. Instead she needed to remember how it felt to be young and in love. It still hurt to see the two of them, but tonight the bride in the home-sewn lace gown looked unfamiliar, a childlike stranger, too naive and vulnerable to be the same woman she was today. In the picture she had an old gold locket hanging from her throat, the one worn by her grandmother on her wedding day. Now a widow confined to a nursing home after a serious stroke, Grandma Kramer was Jennie's favorite person in the world. She found a picture of her taken at the reception in the church basement and felt sad because it was never possible to turn back the clock.

Taking out the album had been a mistake. She was like a person who had crossed a deep chasm on a shaky footbridge of weathered rope, and looking back only made her wonder why she'd been so foolhardy. Whatever the future held, she wanted to make all her decisions based on sound reasoning.

Listening to her heart she'd agreed to another meeting with Matt, but she wouldn't be impetuous again. The past few years had been a time of healing; she was more than wary of receiving new wounds.

Rarely impulsive in her shopping Jennie saw a cream georgette dress in a store window Saturday morning and knew it was going to be hers even before trying it on. Under the neon lights in the dressing room, four graceful tiers, falling from shirred shoulders, swirled around her, convincing her to buy a ready-to-wear dress for the first time in years. Leaving the store with the lovely dress wrapped in tissue in a lightweight gold-and-black-striped box made her feel reckless and extravagant and also very, very feminine. Unfortunately she had to buy shoes to go with it, choosing three-inch bone pumps that made her feel tall and glamorous; fortunately she could carry an Art Deco evening bag made of gold, cream, and orange metal links, handed down in her family but rarely used because it was so exotic.

Her last stop was at a beauty shop, where her hair was styled into an ash-blond helmet, the locks on the sides hugging her cheeks like the tails of two quarter-moons, giving her delicate features a jaunty cast. The day had been dry and balmy; finally she could leave her coat at home, sure that summer was on the way. She was elated at the prospect of seeing Matt again!

Telling him not to call was a mistake she regretted, several times going to the phone herself but never dialing his number, although she looked it up in the phone book enough times to memorize it. By the time eight P.M. came, she was afraid he wouldn't come. She'd tried so hard to discourage him, he might decide not to show up.

Her worries were groundless; two minutes later he was in her living room, looking so handsome in a suit the color of bittersweet chocolate that she was momentarily speechless, not quite believing he was there to be with her.

"All week I've been telling myself you couldn't possibly be as beautiful as I remembered, and here you are: gorgeous."

"You're too kind." She'd never said such a coquettish thing in her life!

"No, just very pleased to be with you."

"I'd offer you a drink, but I can't be late. I have the gift." She picked up her shimmering evening bag and a small box wrapped in embossed gold-and-blue paper.

The party was just getting started in one of the private rooms in the Bancroft Hotel when they arrived. A small band in midnight-blue tuxedoes was tuning up at one end where the carpeting had been removed to reveal a highly waxed wooden dance floor. Martha was standing by the door with her husband, the director of the local branch of Safeguard Health Insurance, his wife, and several other company executives. She hugged Jennie, who was trying to keep the gift out of sight behind her back, and beamed her approval when Matt was introduced.

What a strange sensation, being with a handsome man, introducing him to her friends, seeing the curious and somewhat envious glances of other women, she thought. She'd forgotten how it felt to be part of a couple, to feel wanted and admired instead of being one of the singles, who tended to sit together at tables on the sidelines at office affairs. But she warned herself not to let being part of a twosome color her feelings for Matt. She didn't want to be with him because it was comforting or prestigious or attention-getting.

Tonya was there with Garth Swenson, one of the field representatives. After the two men were introduced, Tonya took her aside for a moment to talk about the gift.

"Smitzer wants to make the presentation. Do you mind terribly?" Tonya asked apologetically. "He will be our new boss starting Monday."

"No, it's all right."

"But you picked it out. You should do it."

"I don't mind. Getting up in front of all these people gives my stomach butterflies." She handed over the gift, thinking how much easier it would be to dance without having to keep track of the package.

"It's not fair. I've got a bad feeling about Smitzer."

"He's well organized. He might not be so bad," Jennie replied.

"As long as we learn to genuflect when he comes into the room!" Lowering her voice Tonya said, "He's tall."

"Smitzer? He isn't much taller than I am."

"Not him! Matt! You were going to save the tall ones for me."

"Matt and I are only friends," Jennie assured her. "You can dance with him."

"No, I wore pokey little heels so I can dance with Garth without looking down on his bald spot."

"He doesn't have one."

"Not from where you stand!"

Matt walked over and took her arm, making her glad Tonya wasn't going to take her up on the offer to exchange dances. Being at the party with a man wasn't the wonderful thing: it was being with Matt.

The band played music from Martha's younger days, dreamy big-band numbers with lyrics about love sung by a tenor, whose voice was still sweet even though his hair was white and wispy.

"Dance with me," Matt invited.

He held her close, tucking her small hand in his larger one, resting his palm low on her back, leading as though they'd danced together for years.

"Could you possibly," he asked in a low voice, "scratch my back?"

She giggled but complied, rewarded by a deep moan when she found the right spot.

"I love to have my back scratched," he admitted, managing to hold her quite a bit closer without making it impossible to move.

"Why do I think you're teasing?"

"You feel safer if you don't admit I'm dying to seduce you." He grinned, not at all ashamed of baiting her.

"Matt!" She stopped dancing. "Are you always so outspoken?"

"It's one of my worst characteristics. Whenever I tell the absolute truth, people laugh or think I'm not serious."

The music stopped, and they followed others back to the tables, sitting down across from Tonya and Garth. The two men discovered several mutual acquaintances, but Matt kept both women in the conversation, enjoying their comments and rarely looking away from Jennie. All her life she'd been used to men who withdrew from feminine companionship, preferring to go off together for endless conversations that established their male bonds. Matt was a different breed, and she was intrigued, wanting to believe he was sincere, but distracted by the pressure of his knee against hers under the table. His words about wanting to seduce her kept hammering in her mind, making her an inattentive listener.

"Don't you agree, Jennie?"

With no idea what Matt was asking, she didn't try to answer.

"You weren't paying any attention," he scolded lightly.

"I'm sorry."

"Don't be. I'd love to know what you were thinking."

She wasn't going to tell him! "What did you ask me?"

"If being a witness to a robbery has made you look over your shoulder more often."

Was Matt trying to warn her that she should? She wasn't used to being protected.

"I suppose it does. In Hopewell no one locks their doors, and you can leave bikes or lawn mowers out all summer and no one will take them. It was hard learning to be defensive here."

The band took a break, and Mr. Smitzer kicked off a round of speeches too affectionate to be a roasting and too personal to leave Martha dry eyed. Watching the fussy little perfectionist who was going to be her new boss made Jennie a little uneasy. Her job was a source of satisfaction, and she was only beginning to realize how much the calm and happy atmosphere of the office was fostered by Martha.

Later, saying good-night to the guest of honor, she urged Martha to keep in touch but knew the Berrys' retirement plans would make it difficult.

"I feel like I've lost a foster mother," she admitted to Matt as they left the hotel.

"She seems like a nice person, but you have me now."

His words were meant to be reassuring, but they stirred up doubts instead. Did he see her as a woman who needed protecting? Was she giving him the impression she needed someone to take care of her?

"Matt, it's too soon to say that."

He put his arm around her shoulders and pulled her close. "I'm used to making quick decisions. My clients can lose thousands of dollars if I hesitate once I recognize a trend in a stock."

"Don't be in a hurry to decide anything about us!"

He laughed, guiding her away from the parking ramp where his car was. "Come on. Let's walk in the park."

One of the nicest features of downtown Burdick was the spacious park in the center, where benches flanked tree-shaded paths and a huge modernistic cement fountain was illuminated on summer evenings. The wooded area with flower beds and the central square were deserted tonight, the big fountain still dry after a winter of being shut down.

"I like dancing with you," Matt said, taking her in his arms and twirling her around on the path beside the fountain.

Hanging her purse on her wrist she laughed and let him guide her across the dark paving and lift her onto the rim of the fountain.

"I've always wanted to do this," he said, jumping ahead onto one of the raised sections of concrete in the center. The fountain was designed to have water shoot over a series of platforms in the form of a pyramid, and they danced on the first rise, laughing with pleasure.

She followed him to the second, swept into his arms, and then to the next, dancing on every level, twirling, dipping, and swaying, climbing higher until, breathless and giddy, they reached the top.

"One more?" He bowed, hugging her against him for a crazy and thrilling dance accompanied by his off-key but delightful humming.

She was in his arms, on the top of a fountain as high as a housetop, kissing him as eagerly as he kissed her.

"I've always wanted to do this!" he repeated fervently, crushing her against him as his mouth covered hers in a demanding kiss that made her dizzy with longing.

"Are you sure this isn't against the law?" she gasped, hanging on to him to keep her balance.

"Feeling this good can't possibly be illegal." He kissed her again, holding her tightly.

"Wouldn't this be fun with the fountain on?"

"Isn't it fun now?" He locked his hands across the small of her back, his fingers sliding lower to squeeze her bottom.

"Matt!"

"We'd better go down before I do get us arrested."

"I'd hate to stand in a lineup."

"I don't think it will come to that," he said, laughing so loudly his voice seemed to resound through the park.

Going ahead he lifted her by the waist, level by level down the pyramid-shaped fountain, letting her length slide against him and claiming a kiss as toll on every drop.

Walking more sedately they went back for his car, laughing like kids at the fun they were having.

"That's the silliest thing I've ever done!"

"Yes, but you loved it," he said, hugging her against him as they entered the gloomy, low-ceilinged interior of the parking ramp.

"I did," she admitted, putting her arm around his waist, loving the slender firmness of his body under her arm.

They were quiet as he drove out of the parking ramp, but the street he took didn't go in the direction of her apartment.

"I promised to drive you past my house," he said when she questioned him.

The street had once been the town's most elegant, and recent efforts had restored much of the Victorian charm of the huge houses. A few contained the offices of agencies like Family Services and the Red Cross, but most were privately owned, converted to apartments without spoiling the original façades. This Matt told her, but she was familiar with the street. His house was one of the grander ones, red brick with dark roof-tiles and stark white gingerbread trim in every conceivable place from the upper windows to the large front porch.

"I'd like to show it to you," he said.

"Maybe I'd better go home tonight and see it another time."

"If you don't want to come inside, at least sit in my porch swing. I just had it installed last month."

"Matt, I don't know."

"A little swinging, and I'll drive you home," he said persuasively.

His swing was as long as a couch, with thin pads on the seat and against the backrest. They sat side by side, holding hands, listening to the rhythmic creaking of the chains fastened into the porch roof.

"This is nice," she said quietly.

"Being with you is nice," he said seriously, taking her hand and laying it on his leg. "It's wonderful."

His thigh was muscular and hard on top, but softer on the inner side when her fingers curled there, first innocently, then self-consciously, but not without an excited sense of pleasure. She tried to pull away, but his hand imprisoned hers.

"It took me nearly three years to redo the whole house." He spoke casually, but they were both uneasy, more so than could be explained by simple arousal. "I renovated the other apartments first to help with the payments."

"Did you do the work yourself?" She freed her hand, holding onto his arm instead because not touching him seemed a deprivation.

"The unskilled stuff like sanding floors and painting. Stripping the woodwork was the worst. Miles and miles of curlicues and scrolls and scallops. I wanted all natural wood, but I finally gave up and repainted it in some of the rooms. Look, this is silly. Come in and see. Then I promise to take you home right away."

"All right."

"I'm proud of the stairway, even if I did have to install a modern door at the top to block off the apartment above. The tenants use the back stairs. There are two other exits, one for family and one for servants originally."

"This is beautiful!" She touched the curving honey-gold oak banister with the tips of her fingers.

"Like everything else in the house it had been painted and repainted, the last time with black paint. It took me a whole winter to get it this way."

The lower floor was even larger than she'd thought from the outside. The old parlor was Matt's living room; the paneled library with built-in shelves was his office and den.

"The kitchen was huge, with a walk-in pantry and a servants' dining room, so I gutted the whole area and divided it into a dining room and a modern kitchen. That way I could make two bedrooms out of the old dining room."

"Your furniture is wonderful. So many antiques."

"I haunted auctions and tag sales for years. My mother once accused me of being married to the house. Now it's just a nice place to live."

She knew it was more than that, and her enthusiasm pleased him immensely.

"It's a good investment," he said.

"It's a beautiful home!"

She didn't go beyond the door of either bedroom, one furnished very sparsely for guests and the other neat and masculine with a huge oak wardrobe and a brass bed with a cover of sheepskin and leather sewn in alternating squares.

When she went into the parlor to admire the pleasant blend of modern rust-colored upholstered pieces and nicely restored antiques, he waited in the doorway. He was going to keep his promise and take her home; she hadn't doubted him.

"I had a wonderful time," she said at her door.

"I'm glad. So did I."

"Did you ever do that before, dance on the fountain?"

He laughed softly. "Never! I used to be your average sober citizen."

"You make a nice lunatic."

"Only when I'm with you." He bent his head and kissed her mouth, but didn't take her in his arms. "Good night, sweet Jennie."

He left, but his words lasted and lasted, caressing her soul like dewdrops on a wild violet.

CHAPTER FIVE

"I've been reviewing some of your cases, Ms. Martin, and I have a feeling on this one." Mr. Smitzer slapped a folder down on her desk as though he expected to swat a fly with it. "I have my doubts about whether Gary W. Post is still eligible to be included on his parents' policy."

Jennie was about to explain that the young man was a college student whose name often appeared on the sports page as a member of a football squad, but it seemed wiser to be diplomatic with her new supervisor. The payoff was a small one for a skin growth removed during the summer break. She could mail out a routine form requesting that the parents verify his status. There was no question about the claim being legitimate, but it was pointless to humiliate her new boss by pointing out that the young man was a football hero with fans all over the state.

"I'll verify his status," she said pleasantly, trying to like the man.

His eyes widened with gratitude behind round lenses held on an elfin face by silver wire frames. "Well, thank you. That will be fine. Thank you."

Watching him retreat from her cubbyhole she was worried that he'd have a very hard time supervising the department. In spite of his balding pate, thinly covered by a few strands of almost colorless hair, and the shrunken appearance of his body, he was still in his thirties and unused to being in charge. Office rumor said he was very intelligent with an M.A. in business, but lack of confidence made him sharp tongued and demanding. He might be a nice person, but he was going out of his way to act like a tyrant.

People were never quite what they seemed, but in the two weeks since the retirement party, Jennie had worried more about the robbery suspect than her new boss. Neil Blockman had been charged of the crime, and there would be a trial, although she didn't know when it would come up on the busy court docket. Testifying was a serious responsibility, one she wasn't at all comfortable facing. Matt said to tell the judge and jury she wasn't sure, just as she had the police, but that seemed like an unsatisfactory way to testify. She desperately wanted to be positive, one way or the other.

Uncertainty colored her personal life, too, but she saw Matt often, almost every other day for lunch or dinner.

Tonight would be the last time they'd be together for a week, since she was going to Hopewell for a vacation, and the day passed slowly in anticipation of seeing Matt. On her way out at five o'clock she reminded Mr. Smitzer about her vacation.

"I'll be gone next week," she said, finding him at his desk in the only enclosed office in the department.

"Oh, yes. I'm sorry you had to take part of your vacation so soon this year. There were some things I wanted you to do next week."

"I haven't seen my family since Christmas," she explained. Nor was she likely to get back to Indiana if she didn't go now. The prospect of being a witness was putting a damper on vacation plans.

Matt met her at the street door with his car, leaving work early himself because they wouldn't see each other for a week.

"How was your day?" He leaned over and brushed a kiss on her lips, unruffled by the blast of a horn behind him.

"The drivers in this town have no romance in their souls," he said, pulling into the stream of traffic.

"Neither does my boss. He doesn't want me to take any vacation time this early."

"Are you still going to?"

"Yes, he didn't say I couldn't. In fact I think he'd like to be nice to people, but he's afraid no one will respect him if he's kind."

"That's too bad. Did you apply for his job when it opened up?"

"No. It was sure to go to someone with a four-year degree."

"They don't teach you how to get along with people in college. You're already a Ph.D. in that department."

She glowed under his compliment, sure that he exaggerated, but enjoying his companionship more each time they were together.

"We're having dinner at my place. You don't mind, do you?"

She didn't.

He made stir fried chicken with mushrooms and vegetables he'd cut ahead of time and stored in plastic bags, serving it on fluffy rice. They drank wine spritzers while he cooked and wine with their dinner, laughing a lot, sometimes forcing it because they were going to be apart. Neither looked forward to any kind of separation.

"Don't go to Indiana," he said as they sat side by side, pretending to watch a cable TV movie in his parlor.

With his arm around her shoulders and their legs stretched out side by side on a hassock, she almost murmured the answer her heart wanted to give. Leaving him for even a day would be painful. Instead she smiled enigmatically and said nothing.

"I'll take the week off too. We'll drive south until we find a place where summer's well under way, maybe Kentucky or Tennessee. Can you imagine how much fun we'd have going through Mammoth Cave together?"

She could, and the thought of long, companionable days and nights spent making love brought bright circles of heat to her cheeks.

"I can't. I have to see my family. My grandmother isn't well, and—"

"Then I'll go with you."

"Would you do that?" She could imagine the excitement if she showed up with a man.

"Sure." He hugged her closer, nuzzling her ear, his breath warm and tickling.

"No, I have to go by myself."

"That's choice, not necessity, isn't it?" He moved his arm away and sat sideways, the doubt in his eyes making it impossible for her to look directly into them.

"I explained last weekend. I need to go away for a while."

If the sadness in her voice touched him, he pretended otherwise.

"You're running away, Jennie."

"A week isn't forever!"

"I hope not." He picked up the TV controller from the Eastlake table beside the couch and turned off the set, replacing the box on the smoky-white marble top.

"You don't like the movie?" she asked.

"Don't tell me you know what was going on."

"No."

The evening was a failure. She'd been nicer to Mr. Smitzer today than to Matt! Every moment with him was precious, but tonight she seemed to have a balloon in her chest holding back a rush of tenderness and desire so potent it could alter her whole life.

"Jennie." He leaned toward her, pushing up her bright-red-and-navy plaid skirt, stroking her knee until an involuntary moan reassured him of the power of his touch.

She couldn't be indifferent to his kisses as his lips took hers, gently at first, then more demanding.

"Let me love you," he urged. "Please."

The rigidity of her body rejected him, but he understood more than she was able to tell him. He gently massaged her shoulders, then his hands moved down to caress the swollen buds of her breasts. Matt was paying a high price for his tender restraint, but he said nothing, gradually pulling away, breathing deeply to gain control.

"Matt, I just need to be alone for a while." Her voice was shaky.

Jennie saw herself in an airplane with skydivers jumping into the void, one after another, leaving her behind because what was easy for them was impossible for her.

"Maybe you're right," he said, but his tone of voice dismissed the possibility.

What was happening between them? When he reached for her hand, she let it rest in his, the caress of his thumb on her wrist telling her things she wasn't ready to hear. The attraction between them was potent; it was easy to believe they were falling in love. Matt urged her to let their feelings take a natural course; he wanted to express his in physical love. To Jennie that required a commitment, and commitment meant no doubts or reservations. Her biggest fear was that she'd fail him as she had Kirk. Some people, she was sure, were natural losers, doing well on their own but bringing unhappiness to people who tried to share their lives. Was she one of them?

"Will you drive me home now?" she asked.

"If that's what you really want." He didn't release her hand, but he did stare straight ahead, as though watching his own fantasy flickering on the screen of the television set.

"I love being with you, but . . ." Not for the first time words failed her.

"Jennie, it's not just going to bed with you." He met her

eyes and smiled sheepishly. "I'd trade my mutual funds to make love to you right now, but you mean more than that to me. A whole lot more."

"I feel the same way," she admitted in a whisper, "but we may not be good for each other—I may not be right for you."

"That's my decision."

"You can't make it alone."

"No, I suppose not," he admitted wearily.

The night was breezy, but they escaped the wind as he followed her down the steps to her door.

"Call me when you get back," he urged.

"Yes, I will."

"It's a long bus ride. I'll still go with you if you want me to."

"I need to go alone, Matt, but I do appreciate your offer. Thank you."

"Maybe you're right. Some time apart might be good." He put his arms around her, looking down on windblown hair turned yellow under the door light. "We can't go on indefinitely the way we are, Jennie. It's up to you whether we go forward."

Or stop altogether, she thought to herself before he gently kissed her, covering her mouth with his.

"Jennie, darling."

She barely caught his words over the sound of the wind, but the emotion in his voice made her wish, just once, she could do a rash, wholly self-serving thing and accept all that Matt was offering: his affection, his eagerness, his lovemaking.

"Good night, my good friend," he murmured into her ear.

"Thanks . . ."

Before she could say "for dinner," he squeezed her shoulder, admonished her to lock up, and left. He was up the stairs and out of sight before she shut herself in for the night.

Crazy! Her legs were trembling as though she'd just stepped off a roller coaster, and she wanted to take back every word she'd ever said about not rushing into an affair. "I didn't mean it," her heart cried out, wanting to tell him the cool cautious woman he knew was an illusion, a poor deluded creature who thought she could deny the hurricane force of newly discovered love.

Moving through the dark apartment she went into her bedroom and sank down on the edge of the bed, tensing every muscle in her limbs until she felt like a giant spring tangled on its own coils. The past was a net trapping her within herself. The young girl who'd naively tied her life to that of an unreliable boy no longer existed, but the old Jennie's fears and failures were indelibly stamped on the consciousness of the person she had become. Before she could reach out to Matt, she had to reach an accord with her own shortcomings and doubts.

Hot tears, the first in many months, ran unchecked down her cheeks as she collapsed in a sobbing heap, crying, not in sorrow or pain, but from confusion. Before she could say yes to Matt, she had to stop saying no to herself. Time didn't heal everything, it only buried the despair under the trivia of everyday living. Happiness was within her reach again, but it was a gamble with high risks and no guarantees. What made it seem so chancy was that Matt could be the big loser.

The bus ride through Indiana lulled Jennie into a restless nap, broken by frequent stops and vivid dreams. This was her favorite time in the country, with long rows of bright-green seedlings following the contours of the land and black puddles of rainwater still standing in the low sections. The closer she got to home the more unbelievable it seemed that a seductively attractive man was interested in her. Perhaps she'd return to find their relationship had far less depth than she'd imagined. Maybe Matt was an accomplished seducer, and she was only an unusually stubborn challenge.

In the depths of her heart she denied this; she didn't doubt his sincerity.

The bus didn't go through Hopewell; her parents were waiting for her at the crossroads two miles from town when she arrived there. Her mother, Nell, a little plumper and grayer than Jennie remembered, welcomed her with tears of joy moistening her eyes. Her father Tom, always reticent, started asking about the bus ride to conceal his pleasure in seeing her. He put her suitcase into the back of his old green Ford station wagon and let the two women squeeze in together on the front seat, not entering into their conversation except to answer a couple of Jennie's questions with one-syllable words.

The white two-story frame house changed little from year to year. It had been dull yellow when they first moved into it, exchanging it for their little two-bedroom cottage across town because she and Josh needed separate bedrooms. Her father painted it white, the "only decent color for a house," the summer before she started kindergarten. She used to wait beside the ancient maple in the front yard for the big bus that took all the town kids to a big regional school. The tree was more than half dead now, with stark-black branches outnumbering the budding ones, but she was glad her father had spared it so far.

Hopewell hadn't changed much either. Her father's hardware store shared a squat gray brick building with the drugstore and barber shop. Because it was Saturday, all the angled parking spaces on Main Street were occupied by farmers' pickups and station wagons, but during the week the broad, bumpy thoroughfare was practically deserted. Her father dropped his women at the house and hurried back to work; he would have done the same on a slower day, because men in Hopewell didn't sit home gabbing when there was work to be done. Before he left, he tousled her hair the way he had years ago and said, "Good to see you." Coming from him it was a speech of welcome.

Her mother had aunts, uncles, cousins, and relatives whose ties were too tenuous to worry about, and all of them would be there for Sunday dinner, a big picnic in the backyard. Being there was the only demand her mother would make on her, but Jennie knew she'd be voluntarily spending every minute until it was time to leave for church peeling potatoes, mixing up cakes and pies, cleaning vegetables, and helping Nell prepare for the onslaught of hungry kin. She didn't mind the preparations; having quiet time with her mother made the chores worth doing, but she wouldn't mention Matt. Her mother's attitude about men was simple: a woman needed one. She couldn't understand why her pretty daughter didn't stay home and take her pick of the available men in the county.

The rest of the week Jennie went to visit her grandmother every day, trying not to be depressed by the tan walls and dark tiled floors that never succeeded in looking anything but institutional. A well-meaning occupational therapist kept paintings, drawings, and handicrafts on display wherever possible, but colorful fabric wall hangings and cute little birdhouses only made the common room seem like a kindergarten for very old children.

They talked about Matt; sharing with her grandmother was easy. Jennie couldn't remember a time when the tiny woman, all her rounded softness lost to the ravages of age, hadn't been her confidant and friend. Children with loving grandparents were especially blessed, Jennie knew. Grandma still listened with keen interest, her mind sharp even though speaking and moving came with some difficulty.

"Is he a good man?" she asked.

"Yes, he is."

Nodding approval she made Jennie describe again how he liked to laugh and tease.

"Men are an awful bother," her grandmother said, "but once in a while one comes along that's worth the trouble."

Her old bike was still in the garage, oiled by her father every fall even though no one had ridden it for years. Every day she pedaled out to the nursing home rather than borrowing her father's car, then followed meandering routes, finding her way home after long rides that left her calves aching, her seat sore, and her mind refreshed. Only once did she ride past the big frame house where she and Kirk had lived. Always shabby, it hadn't been painted since the Martin relatives had readied it for their stay-at-home honeymoon. The green siding was cracked and peeling, scoured season after season by wind, rain, and snow. Mr. Martin liked to say there was nothing between Indiana and the North Pole but a barbed wire fence; he also liked to pretend he'd thought of the witicism himself.

Across a dirt drive, farther from the road, the Martins' yellow ranch-style house, built just before Kirk was born, was nestled in a grove of trees, surrounded by outbuildings and unsheltered farm equipment. Kirk's father was a good farmer; people used to say it was a shame his son hadn't taken to it the same way. With only daughters left, none of them married to farmers and all living some distance away, it was only a matter of time before the farm passed from the Martin family for the first time since an ancestor had cleared the land. Carl Martin would never forgive Jennie for not having produced a grandson to take over when he was gone; he'd never admit it was his son who hadn't been ready to be a parent.

Amanda Martin would want to see her daughter-in-law, but Jennie couldn't bring herself to stop. The only thing they shared now was sorrow. It was time to get on with her life instead of dwelling on the past; her grandmother, weaker every time she came home, was a poignant reminder that everyone was allotted only so much time. It was good to be young, alert, strong, but these were gifts that wouldn't last. Love would. Could she afford to turn her back if there was even one chance in a thousand that she could give Matt as much as he deserved?

She didn't ride past the gloomy farmhouse again, but she thought about it continually. The flowers she'd planted were gone, either mowed, trampled, or lost to neglect. Nothing she'd tried to do there had lasted; even the cheerful gingham curtains in the front windows had been replaced. Could she make a more permanent home for Matt?

She was jumping ahead too fast! He'd never married and hadn't suggested in any way that he might want to someday. His house was practically perfect as it was, and he hadn't even hinted there might be a permanent place for her in his life.

Her last day in Hopewell was a dreary, cloud-shrouded afternoon, but she defied the prospect of rain, going by bike to the country cemetery where the Martin clan was buried, laying a bouquet of her mother's spring flowers on the small square of white granite that marked Kirk's grave. It was a tearless pilgrimage because the misery of knowing she'd failed him couldn't be helped by crying.

The next morning, Saturday, her parents waited at the same crossroads until the bus stopped for her. Being with them had given her time to think. It hadn't given her any answers, but she knew now they'd be found within her, not in a sentimental return to her home.

The trip back was even more monotonous, and she didn't sleep. Seeing familiar places, rethinking all the things that had happened, proved that she could face the past, but it didn't guarantee her future. Admitting to herself that she very much wanted to keep seeing Matt, Jennie still didn't know if she could be the woman he deserved. Admitting she was frightened was a first step, but it seemed an inadequate one.

Jet lag was glamorous, but bus drag was really a test of character, Jennie decided, claiming her bag from the driver in the Burdick terminal. Her face felt powdered by grime and her slacks had pleats across the front and a jelly stain from one of the sandwiches her mother had sent with her in a paper bag. She took a taxi home and made a nonstop dash for the shower, stuffing everything she stripped off except her sandals into the clothes hamper.

Tilting her head back into the spray to rinse away shampoo, she let warm water cascade down her back, beginning to feel fully human again. Clean and relaxed, she didn't try to discipline her thoughts. One person filled them: Matt. Her pilgrimage home hadn't changed anything, but being away had made her miss him to distraction.

Quickly drying and slapping a powder mitt over wellscrubbed pink skin from her throat to her thighs, she dashed into her room and slipped into panties and a short beach-robe of lightweight red terry-cloth. Matt had asked her to call, so after talking to him, she'd decide whether to get dressed or put on a nightgown and robe for what was left of the evening.

Trying to picture how he'd look answering in either his den or bedroom, she was too preoccupied to notice how long she waited. Not willing to believe he wasn't home, she belatedly kept track of six, then seven and eight rings, finally breaking the connection but not giving up. Punching out his number once more in case she'd made a mistake the first time, she again waited in vain to hear his voice.

There was no reason to expect him to sit home waiting for her call, she told herself, trying to gloss over her disappointment. Sitting down on a kitchen chair, she stared moodily at her outstretched legs and bare feet. Where was he? Sometimes he worked at the office on Saturday mornings to catch up on paper work, but he rarely missed playing tennis or racquetball at his club in the afternoon. Possibly he'd gone for dinner with friends and lingered in the restaurant past the time he'd expected her to be back. Maybe the friend he was with was a woman.

Standing abruptly she pushed aside this disturbing thought. No matter what he was doing, she didn't have any right to be jealous or suspicious. She'd insisted on going to Indiana alone, with one very important result: now she could admit to herself how much Matt meant to her.

The sound of the door buzzer brought a wild throbbing to her throat, as though her heart had jumped up and lodged there. Any number of friends could be checking to see if she'd gotten home safely, but her instinct served her well. It was Matt.

"I missed you," he said, stepping into the room with a wistful grin that said it better than words.

"Me too."

What she lacked in verbal eloquence she more than made up in body language, leaping into his outstretched arms and hugging him as though he were the only tree standing in a tropical storm.

"If Indiana affects you this way, I'm going to relocate," he teased, kissing her with a sweet soundness that left her gasping for air.

"I just tried to call you."

"I was on my way here. I couldn't wait to see you." He didn't let go.

"I'm glad you're here." Suddenly aware of her short robe Jennie said, "I'd better get dressed. I just took a shower."

He detained her with a kiss, toying with her lips until they parted, and claiming forcefully what she was so willing to give.

"Did I miss you!" His hands roamed over her back, discovering just how short her robe was.

"I hope so," she said fervently, stepping back to look him over and make sure he was real, not an illusion she'd conjured up in her eagerness to see him.

"Be sure." He brushed a slightly damp tendril from her cheek and trailed his finger to her throat.

"Do you want to sit down or have some dinner or what?"

"None of the above." He reclaimed her in the circle of his arms. "Did you have a nice week?"

"Yes," she said thoughtfully, still trying to sort out the effect it had had on her feelings for him. If possible she cared even more, but realizing this made her even more unwilling to enter into a relationship that might let him down.

"I had a terrible one. The stock market dropped and I didn't even care. All I wanted was to see you again."

"I'm glad." Her eyes teared, but she blinked back the evidence of her emotionalism. "I was ready to get out and push the bus to make it go faster."

Without giving her a choice he propelled her toward the couch and pulled her down on his lap, kissing her again with slow relish.

He was wearing green running shorts, and there was nothing between the pleasing fuzziness of his thigh and hers. She squirmed a bit, embarrassed but excited too. She realized with a start that until then she'd never seen his legs, never felt the skin and firm muscles of them.

"I missed you so much," he said before kissing her again.

She couldn't hear it too often, adding her own longings in a low, husky voice.

His soft knit shirt was bright yellow with a white collar and three buttons at the throat, all of them open. She tucked her fingers under the buttonholes, delighting in the silky hairs that curled around them, caressing warm skin and resting her head against his shoulder.

"Tuesday I nearly got in my car and tracked you down," he said, sliding his hand under the back of her robe, over the little dimpled hollow at the end of her spine, and up the smooth expanse of her back. "Then I changed my mind."

"Why?"

The after-shave on his cheeks was so aromatic it was making her giddy.

"I hoped by the end of the week you'd miss me as much as I was missing you."

"I did," she admitted, feeling more ready for love than ever before.

"I'm going to pick you up," he said in a low, soothing voice.

"Carry me?" She was finding it hard to breathe.

"Yes, to your bedroom. Then I'll untie your robe and slide it away from your shoulders."

"Matt, you're teasing!"

"Not at all. Then I'm going to take you in my arms."

"Oh?"

"And kiss you the way you should be kissed."

His voice made her shiver, but she was beyond protest.

"And make love to you," he whispered.

The promise in his voice was mesmerizing, and she gave her assent by locking arms around his neck and burying her face against his shoulder.

He lifted her easily, slipping his arm under her knees, choosing the right door instead of opening the sewing-room door on the left.

All she felt at first was a floating sensation, as though this moment was preordained, then he let her slide to her toes, keeping his promises as her robe went tumbling to the floor, followed by her panties.

Outwardly she was still as his hands stroked her breasts and waist, his special brand of gentleness far more arousing than forceful caresses. Inwardly her stomach did flip-flops while her heart turned cartwheels. A rush of heat, searing but exhilarating, made her press closer, and she moistened her lips in anticipation of the long, delicious kiss that came as he molded her against his chest. Wanting even more closeness she peeled his shirt upward until he slipped out of it, his muscular flesh firm against the perky mounds of her breasts.

He wore clothes well, but she hadn't expected his body to be so beautiful when he was undressed. His rib cage was prominent above a lean waistline, and his shoulders and upper arms were powerful without being heavy. The few little creases around his middle were endearing, and when he turned to toss aside his shorts, she touched his back, the skin smooth and clear above a hard, nicely rounded rump.

When he pulled her down beside him on the bed, she went gladly, knowing this was the realization of her fantasies, the moment she'd anticipated for many long, lonely nights.

Like two parched travelers drinking together from a deep, cool well, they forgot everything but the delicious relief, letting things happen because giving pleasure was inherent in both their natures. He appreciated being touched, shuddering when she rained feathery kisses on his torso and trailed her fingers from the downy softness under his arms to the hard ridges of his hips. She gave him her trust even as she trembled under seductive kisses and audacious caresses, drawing him close as he parted her thighs.

Words she longed to hear fell from his lips without prompting. "You're beautiful," he whispered. "So beautiful and so special."

Her mind responded, but the words were locked inside. She couldn't begin to say all the things she was feeling. When his deep, loving thrusts grew more frenetic, she was transported to a high plateau, rapture washing over her like a magical wind.

"Special," she murmured, hugging him against her, going limp after he coaxed from her one last tremor of satisfaction.

His cheek rested on the pillow beside her, his lashes long and dark against warm flushed cheeks as he watched her.

"I played a hundred sets of tennis today," he murmured, bringing her fingers to his lips and nibbling on the tips with loving nips. "I wanted to be too tired to seduce you, but it didn't work."

"No one can play a hundred sets," she said, rising to one elbow and leaning over to kiss his forehead. "And this wasn't a seduction."

"Not a one-sided one, anyway," he said gratefully. "I've never met anyone like you, Jennie."

Words were hard for her to bring out, like coaxing water from a rusty pump, but she kissed him again, covering her hesitancy and confusion with very real passion.

"So now will you scratch my back?" He looked at her with a devilish grin and rolled onto his stomach, crossing his arms on the pillow above his head and contentedly closing his eyes.

She loved touching him too much to need any urging. His back was smooth and unblemished, with only a scattering of freckles on his shoulders and a dark little birthmark shaped like an apple below his ribs. Rubbing with her knuckles she worked down his spine, spurred on by his contented moans, then lightly scraped her nails over his shoulders.

"Don't stop," he purred lazily.

His shoulders were slick from the heat of their lovemaking, and she kneaded them with strong, loving fingers, making little circles around his shoulder blades and trailing her nails down the slope of his waist.

"I could lie here forever," he said with satisfaction. "Once more from the top?"

"All you want from me is a backrub," she teased, swatting his bottom.

"All I want from you is you," he said, unexpectedly

whirling over to take her in his arms. "I don't think I've ever been this happy before."

He was too busy kissing her to notice the doubt clouding her eyes. Convinced that happiness never lasted, she wondered what to do to keep from failing him. Hurting him in any way would break her heart.

They had a midnight snack of scrambled eggs because her refrigerator contained little else, eating in the living room, laughing because the sheet he was wearing made a less-than-satisfactory toga.

"Are you going to kick me out?" he asked, only pretending to be flip.

"You want to stay here all night?"

"Do you need to ask?"

She didn't, and nodded because the feeling of closeness between them made her unwilling to examine what had happened that evening.

"Tell me about your vacation," he said, setting aside his plate and putting his arm around her.

"My grandmother isn't well, but we had nice talks every afternoon."

"About what?"

"I told her about you, if that's what you mean."

"I was wondering."

"She thinks men are a big bother."

"Oh?"

"But a good one is worth the trouble." She was saying it more for her own benefit than his.

"Do you agree?"

"Can I get you more coffee?" She leapt up, gathering their empty plates.

"Jennie!" He pulled her down on his lap with a force that was harder on him than her. "Tell me about the rest of your visit." He took the plates away from her and put them back on the table.

"There's not much to tell. Nothing changes in Hopewell. I rode my bike a lot. Dad keeps it well oiled."

"Did you tell your parents about me?"

"No." She squirmed free and slipped to the couch cushion beside him, keeping her legs across his lap.

"They don't want you to be alone the rest of your life, do they?"

"No, just the opposite! If I even mentioned having a friend, my mother would start making plans."

"A friend?"

"Boyfriend sounds a little childish. Gentleman friend is stuffy."

"Try lover," he said, serious under his teasing tone.

"We were talking about my mother!" she said uncomfortably.

"You were telling me about your vacation."

"It wasn't exactly that."

"Did you see friends?"

"A few. Most are married and still feel sorry for me."

"You don't need sympathy anymore?"

Looking into his eyes she saw depths of compassion that assured her of his understanding.

"No. I took flowers to the cemetery." She saw a flicker of pain in his expression and explained, "I said good-bye. It was something I had to do."

He only nodded.

"All my relatives came Sunday," she said, "and I mean all! I have cousins seven times removed. When Mom starts frying chicken, half of the county is our kin."

Laughing, partly in gratitude because the somber moment was past, he gathered her into his arms and kissed her robustly, losing a good part of his toga in the process.

"I am so glad you're back," he said fervently. "The bottom dropped out of my life when you left."

"Oh, Matt, I was only gone a week."

"I wasn't sure you'd come back."

"I did."

"You had to. You'll be subpoenaed for the trial."

"That isn't the reason I'm glad to be back."

"No?"

"Absolutely not." She shook her head and was in his arms again, burying her fingers in thick sable hair and arching her throat for a kiss that led to another and another and another.

CHAPTER SIX

"Take this afternoon off!" Matt's voice was insistent.

"Are you phoning from your office?" She lowered her voice; Mr. Smitzer was crusading against personal calls during working hours.

"Yes, but I'm ready to skip out if you are."

"I don't see how I can."

"Have a headache. A dentist appointment. A sick aunt."

"Matt!"

"Then tell the truth: it's a beautiful day and wasting it at work is a crime against romance."

"I can see myself telling that to Smitzer!"

"I'll tell him."

"And get me fired? No thanks."

"Have you ever missed work for a frivolous reason?"

"No, I haven't even taken a sick day in the last year."

"Tell him you have urgent personal business. I'll pick you up in front at noon."

"You're serious, aren't you?"

"Absolutely."

Mr. Smitzer's ears got very pink below the whispy tuffs of colorless hair that stuck out above them. "I'll have to see what the policy handbook says about emergency time off," he said pompously.

Feeling more than a little guilty she nearly told him not to bother, but the excitement in Matt's suggestion was contagious. "I'll take the afternoon without pay," she said, "and then there can't be any problem."

It was a grand gesture, and one she could ill afford, but her conscience was at peace. She was standing in front of the building when Matt stopped his car by the curb.

"You didn't have any trouble getting away?" he asked as she slid in beside him.

"None I'm going to worry about!"

He drove to her apartment and left her with orders to change into something casual as quickly as possible, but he wouldn't even hint at how they were going to spend their stolen afternoon. When he returned in a short time, she was wearing white shorts, a red-and-white candy-striped shirt with the sleeves rolled to her elbows, and white tennis shoes, feeling jaunty and adventuresome and very, very carefree.

"You look great!" he said, looking terrific himself in khaki shorts and a white knit top. "Put your key in your pocket and let's go."

"First tell me where we're going."

"No. You'll have to trust me."

"Matt, tell me!"

"Come on. I'll show you."

The tandem bicycle was parked at the top of her stairs, sleek and shiny blue.

"I love bikes, but I've never ridden one of these!"

"I borrowed it from my third-floor tenants."

"The married couple with the orange VW?"

"Yes, this is how they spend their weekends in the summer."

"Who gets to ride in front?"

"We'll take turns. You can go first if you know the way to Leiden Park."

"I've never even heard of it."

"Then hop on the back, sweetheart. Lunch is in the basket."

They laughed the first few blocks, getting used to their playful conveyance. She was thankful for her long rides during the week in Indiana, pedaling with ease at the same rate as Matt. Eventually they left the city behind, traveling down a narrow, paved suburban road with older houses scattered on either side. In front Matt's legs moved with a steady rhythm, muscles bunching at the back of his powerful calves. His hair was blowing back from his forehead, the deep brown strands an even richer color when they rode out of a shadowy, tree-lined stretch into bright sunlight.

Houses were farther apart here, and they passed an orchard, the blossoms on the trees nearly gone but the ground still white with petals that fell like snow.

"Not too much farther," he called back, smiling at her over his shoulder.

Being a little hungry was a small price to pay for the joy of watching Matt, his body lithe and strong as he threw himself into the cycling. His shirt was sticking to the skin between his shoulder blades, and she was beginning to feel the sun, too, her arms turning pink and her hair sticking moistly to the back of her neck.

"My family used to hold reunions out here when I was a kid," he said.

"Do they still have them?"

"No, we're too scattered. Since my parents moved to Arizona, I'm the only hometown boy in the family. I miss those big get-togethers. Used to love playing with my cousins when I was a kid."

"Girl cousins?" she teased.

"Yup. Twins. They had red pigtails. I wanted to tie them together back to back by their braids, but I never got the chance."

"What a bully!"

"They could more than take care of themselves! We turn left up ahead."

He called for a halt after riding a few hundred yards on a rough dirt road that was only two tire tracks with high grass in between.

"This is so bumpy, maybe we'd better walk the rest of the way. I don't want to take any chances with a borrowed bike."

He dropped his feet to the ground and got off the seat, stepping aside and rubbing his rear. "I'd forgotten how hard this sport can be."

She laughed and asked, "How long since you've ridden?"

"Ten years, maybe more."

"You did this just for me!" She dismounted and went up to him, standing on tiptoes to plant a kiss on the end of his nose.

"Don't make me sound noble. I'd hang-glide across Lake Michigan to spend an afternoon like this with you."

He steadied the cycle with one hand and circled her waist with the other, nudging her lips apart with his tongue and kissing her slowly and thoroughly.

"Have you ever done that?" she asked, catching her breath as they started to walk.

"What?"

"Hang gliding."

"Not for a million dollars! I don't like heights."

He made her feel so special, so valued, she didn't know how to handle his compliments. The most natural way to say thank-you was to put her arm around his waist and hug him for all she was worth.

The track became more rutted, with a thick woods on either side, as Matt pushed the cycle and she walked beside him.

"I don't remember it being this far," he said. "Maybe because I always came by car."

The tracks curved to the right, then angled to the left,

nding abruptly in a grassy clearing beside a sparkling sapphire lake.

"It's beautiful! Are you sure this is a public park? It seems so hidden and private."

"I'm sure it's not. The Leiden Corporation keeps it for their employees. My uncle used to work there. That's why we were able to reserve it for reunions."

A dozen or so picnic tables were scattered by iron grills, and an area to the left had swings, play equipment, a ball diamond, and a volleyball court.

"Is it all right to be here?"

He laughed. "I don't think anyone will come to challenge us. If they do, I played on the high school tennis team with the vice-president in charge of marketing. He won't mind if I say we're his guests. Anyway, this is a working day. We have it to ourselves."

"You make it easy to forget I should be processing claims!"

He left the tandem by a tree and took their lunch from the basket along with a folded piece of bright-green cloth that turned out to be a practically new bed-sheet.

"It was all I could find in a hurry," he said. "I hope you don't mind bologna and cheese with mustard."

"Anything will taste good today. I'm starved."

They spread the sheet close to the thin strip of sand near the lake and ate the warm, soft sandwiches, hunger making them seem tasty, and washed them down with orange soda in cans.

"I didn't plan this ahead of time," he explained unnecessarily. "I just grabbed a few things I had on hand. Have a fig bar."

"It's the worst lunch I've ever had," she teased, "and the best!"

No one came while they ate, and Matt said the absence of canoes on the lake meant the Y camp on the other side hadn't started their first session of the summer.

103

"We should have brought swimsuits," she said idly, lying on her stomach beside him and watching the play of light sparkling on the water.

"You wouldn't want to swim here. The bottom is all weeds and muck, and you have to wade a long way to deep water." He rested his arm on her waist, moving closer so their bodies touched from hips to toes.

"This is still a good idea. It's like being out on the school playground when all the other kids are doing arithmetic."

"Or finding participles. I still don't know what a participle is." He leaned over and nuzzled her ear, tickling her with his warm breath.

"My favorite subject was spelling. I won the district spelling bee in the sixth grade."

"Spell delectable."

She did.

"Try luscious."

"Too easy. Try me on something hard."

"All the words that describe you are easy to spell: *cute, yummy, gorgeous, sexy* . . ."

"That's enough," she said, laughing.

Rolling on her side to see him better, she wanted to believe their special closeness meant as much to him as it did to her. His eyes were the nicest she'd ever seen; like mirrors of his soul they were open and honest, affectionate and caring. On impulse she touched his lashes, letting each delicate spike brush the tip of her finger. He didn't even blink, waiting until she explored the feathery fringe over each eye before taking her in his arms for a long, languid kiss.

"I'm going to take a nap," he murmured, slowly moving away and lying on his stomach, his head cradled on his arm.

"Do you want me to scratch your back?"

"Don't you dare. I can't be responsible for what would happen."

"I didn't mean—"

"Your hair isn't long enough for braids, is it?"

"You're a terrible tease!" she accused him, her cheeks pink with embarrassment. "I wouldn't dream of . . . not here—"

"I would! That's why I'm going to take a nap," he said, lifting his head just enough to see her.

The ground was lumpy; grass tickled her toes and something with lots of tiny legs crawled over the back of her knee, but she wiggled in contentment, dropping off to sleep without any intention of doing so.

The surface of the lake was so bright she had to squint to look at it, but the glare roused her quickly, her movement waking Matt.

"We both slept."

"No, I'm sure I was awake," he said groggily. "I saw you take off all your clothes and walk toward the middle of the lake."

"I never left your side. You were dreaming."

"Then I'd better go back to sleep so I won't miss your dive."

"Matt!" She shook his shoulders. "It's time to go."

"I meant to pack dinner, but all I had was canned chili." He grinned and slowly got to his feet, offering his hand to pull her up. "This wasn't much of an outing, was it? Bologna sandwiches and a date who falls asleep."

"I loved it," she admitted, looking away so he wouldn't think she was foolishly sentimental.

"So did I." He stepped up from behind and put his arms around her. "I'd rather do nothing with you than do anything else with anyone else."

"I'll have to think about that sentence!"

"Think while you pedal. It's a long ride back, and you get the number one seat."

"I'm not sure I know the way."

"Don't worry. I'll be watching you every minute. I've had my nap."

The ride back seemed longer, mainly because they had to contend with rush-hour traffic once they reached the outskirts of the city.

"I hate to have our day end," he called out as they cautiously rode down a busy street."

"It's been fun, Matt. It really has."

They went through the back parking lot, wheeling the tandem through the arch to her front entrance, not paying any attention to the blue sedan parked at the curb. The driver left his vehicle as soon as Jennie started down her stairs, laughing at something Matt said. Before she could open the door and look up to thank him for his good idea, a square-jawed man with a steel-gray brush cut and a navy suit walked up to them.

"You're Jennifer Elizabeth Martin?"

No one had ever called her anything but Jennie; she looked at him blankly for a moment, then gave an affirmative answer.

"This is a subpoena. You've been duly served."

She unfolded the crinkly sheet of paper, knowing what it was but not quite able to believe it was actually in her hands.

"He should have one for you too," she said to Matt as the man walked away. "Tell him who you are."

"I got mine at the office."

"This morning?"

"Yes."

"What time?"

"Just before I called you."

"Is that why you asked me to take off from work?"

"Let's go inside."

"No. First tell me why you didn't mention getting your subpoena."

"I planned to. I was coming into your apartment now to do it."

She opened her door, not sure how she felt about his subpoena coming first.

"I don't understand why you didn't tell me right away."

He closed the door but stayed near it. "I wanted to prepare you, but it was so nice being with you . . ."

"There was no reason to keep it secret. What did you think I'd do?"

"All right, it was dumb. I thought we could have a nice afternoon, then come back here and I'd mention it casually. I didn't know he'd be waiting for you here."

"There's nothing casual about keeping it secret. That makes a big deal out of it."

"Jennie, you're making too much of the whole incident! There was a crime. You tell them what you saw, and that will be the end of it."

"You're sure Neil Blockman is guilty." She read the date on the subpoena, sorry the trial wasn't scheduled the next day so she wouldn't have to agonize over it for long. "I don't know if he is or not."

"Then say so!" he said impatiently. "You're not the judge and jury. You're getting too excited about this, Jennie. All you can do is say what you think."

"You've said that before. Aren't you worried you could be wrong? What if you say he's the one and he's innocent? Wouldn't that bother you at all?"

"It would bother me a whole lot. But what am I supposed to do? I think Blockman is the man I saw putting on the ski mask. Do you want me to lie about it?"

"No." She didn't know what she wanted.

"I was afraid you'd be upset when the subpoena came. That's why I wanted you to leave the office before the man came to serve it. I thought we could talk it over."

"There's nothing to talk about! You don't want me to identify him if I'm not sure, do you?"

"That's not fair, Jennie! You know I don't."

"I'm sorry." Apologizing didn't make her less upset.

"I don't understand why you're so nervous. Is it getting on the stand that frightens you?"

He came close and put his hands on her shoulders, but she moved away, still looking at the paper in her hands.

"I'm afraid of making a mistake."

He silently watched her, his expression neither censoring nor understanding.

"You could be making one yourself," she said quietly.

"Maybe. But I can't change the way I feel just because there's a chance things could go wrong."

Suddenly they weren't talking about the trial, but it was the worst possible moment to sort out her feelings for him.

When she didn't answer, he asked, "Would you like to have dinner with me?"

"Not tonight, Matt."

"I'll go now, but I hate to leave you like this."

"It's something I'll have to work out myself."

"I know you've had to solve your own problems in the past, Jennie, but I'm here now if you need me."

"That's nice to know," she said softly, knowing how good it would feel to lean on him but unable to do it. No matter how difficult, there were some things she had to handle herself.

He left, but his arguments stayed behind, making her miserable and uncertain of herself and her testimony. Matt was a success in the investment business, a professional person. Compared to what she did, being an investment specialist required a lot of education and intelligence. She couldn't dismiss the possibility that he'd been more alert that morning in the jewelry store. He wouldn't be careless about identifying a man; everything she knew about him affirmed this. Did that mean she was wrong? Was her memory of the thief's face hazy because she was afraid of sending him to prison? Which came first, she thought ruefully, fear or doubt? It was like arguing about chickens and eggs and just about as pointless. The only positive fact was that she was uncertain, if uncertainty could be called a fact.

Screaming inwardly, she made preparations to take a shower, wishing she could skip ahead a few weeks when the trial would be over. The time sacrificed would be very small compared to the long jail sentence Neil Blockman faced, but she couldn't honestly say he wasn't the thief.

The late evening news covered one crisis after another, bringing her an electronic message: there were worse dilemmas in the world than hers. Paying little attention to the button she was sewing onto a doll dress, she pricked herself with the needle, watching in surprise as a tiny bead of blood formed on her finger, just enough to stain the material. She put aside her work and went to rinse the insignificant puncture, but she kept thinking about the importance of her problem. It wasn't earthshaking; the world wouldn't become a better place because she testified in a felony trial. Matt was right about doing her duty, but she couldn't be as casual about it as he was. No matter how hard she tried to stop worrying, the fact remained: people could be wrongly hurt if her account of the robbery was inaccurate. The Garbers and the whole community had a right to expect a dangerous thief to be imprisoned, if Neil Blockman was that man.

This time her late-night visitor didn't surprise her.

"Am I too late for the news?" he asked, closing her door behind him.

"You can catch the sports," she said, stepping close but turning her head so his kiss missed her mouth.

"Are you going to turn the other cheek?" His voice was unusually edgy.

"Sit down," she offered stiffly. "You're just in time for baseball scores."

"The only score I'm interested in is yours and mine."

He walked over to her portable TV and turned it off. "I know you're worried, and I've been trying to figure out why."

"Have you?" Her coolness was a defense, and she wasn't proud of it.

"No. But I've decided it shouldn't matter between us. Pretend you don't even know me in the courtroom, but don't let the trial be a problem between us."

"I can't be sure the way you are. One of us has to be wrong, and you're not even considering the possibility that it's you."

He shrugged his shoulders. "If there's any way I can help you—"

"No," she interrupted. "I'll have to work it out myself."

"But it won't break us up, having different opinions?"

"Matt, I'm not taking sides in this."

"I shouldn't have put it that way, but you know we'll be helping different sides in the trial."

"Maybe we shouldn't talk about it."

"If that's what you want." He sounded mildly hurt.

"I don't know what I want! That's the part I hate!"

"Jennie, anything that bothers you is a problem for me too."

"Oh, Matt, sometimes you're so sweet." She put her arms around him and pressed her cheek against the front of his shirt.

"I can't quite believe it's happened to me, but I love you, Jennie. I really love you."

Jennie suddenly realized she felt the same way, but she couldn't say the words, even though hearing them from him meant so much. It was the wrong time. Squeezing her eyes shut, she held back burning tears and pressed her body against his, trying to liberate her feeling of love from the frustration of knowing it could be inadequate.

"Let me stay," he said softly.

She didn't answer, but he took her silence for assent, stroking her hair and murmuring endearments.

"There're a lot of good things ahead of us," he promised, gently kissing her.

"I hope so." She couldn't get close enough, hugging him as though her life depended on it.

"Don't hope. Just believe." His kiss was more emphatic as he held her swaying in his arms.

Being held gradually coaxed her into a dreamy, acquiescent mood. His lips pressed against her forehead and lingered on her lids, then bedeviled the tip of her nose, making her giggle until he silenced her with a kiss that sent liquid heat racing through her body. His fingers circled her throat, tenderly caressing the satiny skin, his thumbs finding the throbbing pulse and resting there. His voice seemed to come from a great distance, charming her with words that washed over her consciousness like intimate caresses.

Letting her hands creep under his shirt, she ran seeking fingers over the warm expanse of his back, loving the smooth tautness of his skin. Their knees and thighs touched as he lifted her, locking her torso against his as her toes lost contact with the floor and dangled against the tops of his shoes. Sliding down until she was again standing on tiptoe, she felt dizzy with desire, remembering all too vividly how it felt to lie in his arms.

When he turned out the light in the living room, she trusted him to guide her down the dark hallway to her room.

A glow from the lights illuminating the parking lot filtered into her bedroom through filmy gold curtains, but Matt reached up and lowered the shade, making the darkness total. She caught his hand before he succeeded in finding the switch on her bedside lamp.

"I like being able to see you," he said.

"Not this time," she pleaded.

"Come here."

The darkness made their kiss a thing apart from the reality of their lives, and that was what Jennie craved. Her longing grew with wild leaps under his thrilling caresses, and the slow, groping removal of their clothes brought an eagerness she hadn't believed possible.

Tumbling to the bed, thwarting each other in a hasty scramble to remove the spread and blanket, they sorted themselves from the binding covers with bursts of laughter that held more urgency than humor, both of them aching for fulfillment. Through minutes of sweetest agony they suffered a mutual rush of passion, running their hands over throbbing flesh and kissing with the force of a boiling volcano. His skin was hot against hers, adding to the heat of her fever, and both of them were frantic for closeness, for oneness, for a sweeping, joyful union.

His hands were strong on the tender swell of her thighs, and her heart raced out of control when he made a ritual of discovering the moist, silky triangle above them. Writhing under him, undulating in a frenetic rhythm, she was stunned by exploding rockets, overcome by a rush of heat so intense it froze her in time and space, shaking the foundation of her being. Something lost was regained; something never known was revealed. She understood what it meant to be possessed by love.

Hugging him against her breasts she let joy wash over her, trying to hang on to it but finally settling for an exhausted contentment. Her own sexuality, denied and contained for so long, gave her great physical release, but as Matt freed her from the burden of his weight, her mind buzzed with whispered warnings: there was more to happiness than warm, exciting lovemaking.

"I'm still shaking," he admitted with a small, self-conscious laugh.

She wanted to tell him what a wonderful, beautiful man he was, more than any woman could imagine wanting, but she'd never said anything like that. Finding words was scary; her thoughts were hard to translate.

"You're very nice," she managed to whisper.

"Nice?" He leaned over her, gently stroking her cheek. "Terrific."

"I love you," he said, reaching across her to turn on the small lamp.

His face, close to hers, glistened in the bluish glow coming through the fabric shade, and again she thought *beautiful* was the only word to describe the kind, generous, loving light in his eyes. Growing uncomfortable under his long, searching stare, she reached up and traced the outline of his lips, finding them as soft and swollen as her own.

"Someday," he said solemnly, "I'm really going to know you."

"That sounds ominous."

"No, but I don't think our lives are ever going to be quite the same after this."

Hers wouldn't, she knew.

"Better set your alarm for six," he said. "I have to go home for clothes."

Attention to this prosaic detail broke the spell, but Jennie was glad he fell asleep first. When she whispered his name without getting a response, she cuddled against his back spoon-style, wanting to absorb his warmth and strength and sureness.

He awoke before the alarm rang, teasing her into sleepy compliance, but it wasn't the same as the night before. Too many doubts had tramped through her mind as she lay trying to fall asleep.

"Sleepyhead," Matt chided, resetting the clock for her before he left. He kissed her cheek, gave her a noisy lovetap on her bottom, and left.

The apartment was empty without him.

She made coffee and showered, then made a stab at eating a bowl of cold cereal.

Matt said he loved her.

She should be totally happy.

Her bed had never been so rumpled. She changed the sheets and straightened the bedroom. It was too early to dress for work, but she thought of going early to the office. Taking off an afternoon had put her behind.

Suddenly she was sobbing, her crying binge triggered by the thought of Matt spiriting her away to the little unswimmable lake. She was in love, too, so why wasn't she happy? That was the trouble: Matt had brought joy and zest back into her life at a time when she was still cautiously feeling her way back to normality. How could she possibly sort out her own feelings when she was so worried about being less than he deserved? And while she struggled with her conscience and felt inadequate in this new relationship, she had a court case hanging over her head.

Life had seemed so simple and pleasant the first time she fell in love; now she was racked by turmoil, torn between following Matt's lead in everything, even in identifying the thief, and painfully sorting out her dilemmas.

A cold, wet cloth helped the swelling around her eyes, but she didn't know any quick remedy for confusion in the heart.

CHAPTER SEVEN

"I may have done something awful," Tonya said, following Jennie into the elevator to go to lunch.

They weren't alone; several people from the firm on the floor above were in the car too.

"I'll tell you at lunch," she added.

"Why are you being mysterious?" Jennie asked as they left the building to go to the cafeteria across the street.

"You're going to think I'm a terrible gossip!"

"Tonya! Tell me."

"One of my sister's friends had a jewelry party. I really didn't want to go, and wouldn't you know it, I got talked into buying a string of jade beads. It ruined my budget for this month."

They crossed with the light, and Jennie quizzed her friend again. "Is that the terrible thing you shouldn't have done?"

"I wish! There was no one there I knew—only my sister and her friend. If I'd just kept my big mouth shut!"

"Look how long the line is," Jennie said as they entered the busy cafeteria. "Do you want to wait or try the sandwich shop?"

"Let's stay here. It'll move fast, but maybe you won't want to eat with me after you know what I've done."

"Either tell me now or forget it!"

"Well, I'd better tell you. After the sale we had coffee

115

and a dessert with pineapple and almonds and whipped cream."

"The special today is chicken pot pie, if you want to talk about food," Jennie said, reading the menu board, giving up on ever hearing her friend's big story. "I had it once and it's all gravy."

"This is serious, Jennie."

"All right, but don't bother with the part about having dessert."

"We were talking. Eve, the woman selling the jewelry, was telling about the company's security policies. You know, how to protect the samples she had to carry. I casually mentioned having a friend who was in the store when Garber's was robbed, and a woman named Corliss was really interested. She kept asking me questions about you."

"Why was she so interested?" Jennie was getting a little impatient, both with the long line and her friend's long story.

"That's the bad part. She works with Neil Blockman's sister at the hospital. In food service. They're good friends."

"Did you tell her my name?"

"I'm afraid so. Before I knew about her friend."

"Well, I guess it's no secret. The trial will probably be written up in the newspapers."

"She told me a few things." Tonya lowered her voice to a whisper. "His sister is going crazy trying to prove he's innocent. She's borrowed money for a lawyer because she doesn't trust public defenders. Her brother's been in trouble before, so she's had experience. She's hanging out in bars trying to find someone who looks like her brother. According to her friend she practically raised her younger brother, and she'll do anything to prove he's innocent."

"Does she have any proof?"

"I don't know, but I may have mentioned you're not positive about identifying him."

"May have?" Now she did feel cross with Tonya but tried not to show it.

"Let me get your tray." Tonya stepped ahead and picked up two orange ones. "The line did move fast."

"Why do I think you're not telling me everything?"

"Let's get our food first."

Jennie slid a chef's salad from the glass shelf and hurried ahead to get her iced tea and secure a table for two, but Tonya was slow in following.

"I thought you'd deserted," Jennie said.

"No, I waited for a fresh pan of sole. You're waiting to hear the rest, aren't you?" She set her tray on the table and sat down.

"Yes."

"Corliss, that's the friend of my sister's friend who's a friend of—"

"Tonya!"

"Yeah, I'm stalling. His sister will probably come to see you, now that she knows where you work."

"Oh, no! What can I say to her?"

"Maybe it's illegal, harassing a witness," Tonya suggested.

"This is terrible."

"Well, I did think you'd want a warning. I guess his sister is on a rampage. You can always call the police if she threatens you."

"I'm not worried about that. She'll want me to help her brother, and I don't know how!"

"Jennie, I'm sorry."

"Matt says it's a small town when you've lived here a long time. I suppose she could have found out anyway."

"How is Matt?" Tonya asked, eager to change the subject.

She shook her head dejectedly, picking at her salad to avoid looking at Tonya.

"You really should save the tall ones for me," her friend quipped, unsuccessfully trying to lighten Jennie's mood.

They were both quiet walking back to the office.

Jennie sometimes interviewed clients in person if they had special problems with their claims, but it wasn't an everyday part of her job. When a woman came into her partitioned area later that afternoon, Jennie smiled automatically and asked how she could help her.

"By telling the truth about my brother!" The woman's voice was strident, carrying beyond Jennie's cubbyhole. "I'm Wanda Ackerman, Neil Blockman's sister."

"Sit down, won't you?" Jennie asked quickly.

"Neil isn't guilty of anything. You never saw him put on a ski mask." She gripped the edge of the desk but didn't sit.

"I'm not sure I should talk about it," Jennie said.

"Why not, unless you're hiding something?" Wanda Ackerman's voice wasn't pleasant, and although she had good features, they didn't quite add up right. She was lean and angular with hair that was silky but mousy brown. Her large green eyes might look stunning with the right makeup, but she wore none, not even trying to soften the heavy sprinkling of freckles on her face. Her mouth was her least promising feature, small and thin-lipped, unattractively curling around her words.

"Please sit," Jennie urged, hoping she'd lower her voice.

"No, I don't want to hear a lot of wishy-washy bull. Did you see my brother rob that store or didn't you?"

"I'm not sure."

"You can't be not sure! He wasn't there. You couldn't have seen him. He was home in bed. He lives with me and my husband, so I should know."

"Then you can testify that he was home." Jennie sighed with relief, glad someone could be positive.

"No." There was sulkiness in Wanda's reluctance to answer. "It was my weekend to work."

"Your husband—"

"Wasn't home either."

"I have to say what I think."

"You have to tell the truth!" the woman shouted. "If you lie, my brother will go to Jackson Prison. He's only nineteen! He doesn't belong there!"

"Is there a problem, Ms. Martin?" Mr. Smitzer approached her desk and frowned at Jennie.

"No, thank you."

"It's not your problem, is it?" Wanda cried. "My brother's life will be ruined, but it's no skin off your nose!"

"Miss, if this isn't company business, I'll have to ask you to leave," Smitzer said tersely.

"Please, couldn't we talk about this quietly after I get off work?" Jennie begged her visitor.

"You'll have to go!" her boss said emphatically to the intruder.

"Neil didn't rob that store! You're the criminal if you say he did!"

"Really, Ms. Martin, you can't conduct personal business here!" her supervisor reprimanded her.

Jennie ran. Not since she'd first begun working there had she hid in the rest room to cry, and then Martha had tactfully overlooked her grief-stricken lapses. Now she had to wash her face and go have it out with Smitzer.

The rest of the afternoon was a total loss. Her unsympathetic boss wouldn't admit that the "unruly disturbance" hadn't been her fault, and the rest of the department was buzzing over the incident. Jennie practically ran to the elevator at five o'clock.

Matt called shortly after she got home.

"Mind if I come over?"

"Yes! I mean, now isn't a good time. I'm going out for a while."

"If you have things to do, I'll be glad to drive you."

"No, thank you. I really have to be by myself for a while."

"Jennie, you sound upset."

"No, I just have a few things to do. I'll talk to you later."

"I wish you'd let me help."

"Matt, no!"

Knowing she'd behaved badly, she still couldn't bring herself to call him back and apologize. She changed into white cotton slacks and rubber-soled shoes and walked until she felt like dropping.

Neil Blockman was nineteen years old, exactly her age when she'd agreed to marry Kirk. She'd helped ruin Kirk's life, and now she could help destroy another young man if her testimony unjustly sent him to prison.

As she walked along the city streets, loneliness stalked her, making her feel unusually vulnerable. Jennie knew she could be with Matt, but he was part of the problem, not the solution. How could he be so positive about everything: what he saw, what he felt for her, and what he'd say on the witness stand? Was it arrogance or confidence that made him think he had all the answers?

Maybe she wasn't being fair to him or herself. All he'd ever done was try to love her; maybe she was, after all, unlovable.

Everything was all muddled together in her mind: feelings for Matt, tenseness about testifying, and her fear of being wrong. How would Matt feel if she got on the witness stand and contradicted his identification? He said it didn't matter, but would he be so easygoing if he were proved wrong?

She couldn't do that, not because it might ruin their relationship, but because she wasn't sure what she had seen that morning in the jewelry store. Maybe even then her mind had been on the handsome stranger beside the ring counter.

Her thoughts were on a merry-go-round, spinning dizzily but getting nowhere. She had to come to terms with herself first.

Her feet hurt, and her stomach rumbled for food, but Jennie walked on, beginning to see familiar landmarks: the library, the building where a co-worker lived, the street that led to Matt's.

When, at last, she stepped into her living room, the phone was ringing. She didn't answer it.

The next day began smoothly; Mr. Smitzer was practically cordial, and she managed to clear up several cases that had been pending for an unusually long time. Being busy was a blessing, but missing Matt was misery. By late afternoon she had decided to call him.

"Nichols," he said, taking the call on his private line.

"Matt, do you have time to talk for a minute?"

After a long pause he said, "A minute won't begin to cover what we have to discuss. Can I pick you up after work?"

"All right."

They had dinner at the Depot, a restaurant in a renovated brick building that had housed a waiting room in the days of heavy train travel. Unlike some dining places that depended on historical interest for business, the Depot had excellent food. They both ordered the special of the day, pecan-stuffed chicken with wild rice, and ate with the concentration of two people determined to make it seem like an ordinary meal. Jennie's appetite failed first, and she had to say something about Wanda Ackerman.

"The reason I couldn't talk to you yesterday . . ." she began hesitantly.

"I was hoping we'd get to that."

"I guess I'd better tell you. Neil Blockman's sister came to see me."

Matt frowned. "She shouldn't have done that."

"She thinks her brother is innocent, but she's really

frightened. She thinks he's only being blamed for the jewelry-store robbery because he's been in trouble before. Matt, he's only nineteen!"

He shook his head sadly. "You're suffering too much over this witness business. It's up to the jury to decide whether he's guilty. The prosecutor will have other evidence, and Blockman's lawyer will look out for his rights. That's the way it works."

"Isn't there any doubt in your mind?"

"Maybe we shouldn't talk about it. I don't want to influence you."

"But why are—"

"No. You're a mature adult. You have to put this in perspective, Jennie."

"Do you know how pompous that sounds?" She twisted the cloth napkin in her lap, torn between envying his relaxed attitude and finding it callous.

"Jennie, I want to talk about you and me. Is this trial going to come between us?"

"I don't want it to."

"At least we agree on that! No matter what the jury decides, we'll have done our duty."

"Then you won't be upset if he's found not guilty?"

"Only if I think the jury's made a mistake."

"Your testimony will decide them."

"Maybe. They might decide I'm mistaken."

"But you don't think you are?"

"Honey, we're talking in circles. Are you ready to leave?"

Outside the apartment she fumbled with her key, too conscious of Matt standing behind her to concentrate on anything else. Her living room was warm and stuffy after being closed all day; she couldn't afford to run the air conditioning when she wasn't home. Matt volunteered to open the living room window, reaching up to turn the handle that cranked it open.

"Basement living," she said listlessly.

"You've done a lot with it." He gestured at the large hooked rug hanging above her couch, an Egyptian design in shades of brown, gold, and orange, and the mounds of coordinated pillows.

"Thank you. Would you like coffee?"

"No." He shook his head. "I'd like to go back to where we were before the subpoena."

He moved across the room to stand very close, looking down at her with a wistful, musing expression.

"The subpoena hasn't changed anything," she said, not sure it was true. "You didn't need to take me on a bike trip to put off the time when I'd get it."

He shrugged, telling her it wasn't something he wanted to debate. Putting his hands on her shoulders he slowly lowered his head, brushing his lips across hers.

Turning her head she stepped away. "I think I will make some coffee."

"You don't want any." He followed her toward the kitchen. "What are you trying to prove by avoiding me, Jennie?"

"Nothing—I'm not."

He was right; she didn't want coffee.

"Then kiss me," he challenged, catching her in his arms.

"Please . . ." Her protest died as his mouth descended, planting a gentle, chaste kiss on her closed lips.

"Please what?"

"Not right now." She tried to wiggle free, but he held her.

"There's never a wrong time to let you know how much I care about you." His next kiss lasted much longer, his tongue stroking the soft membrane of her mouth, his hand covering one breast until it ached with pleasure.

He'd left his suit jacket in the car, and the front of his white cotton shirt didn't completely conceal the dark, silky hair under it. She drank in his masculine aura, feeling a dangerous tremor as his hands slid over her hips, creating shivers of longing in their path.

"Not tonight," she protested, finding his languid caresses sweet and tempting but not compelling enough to overcome her reservations.

"Why not tonight?"

He slid his hand between her legs, his gentle fondling creating havoc but not overcoming her reluctance.

"Matt, no!"

Vigorously pushing him away she succeeded in stopping his amorous advances, but doing so made her feel a little foolish. Their relationship had passed the point of coy skirmishes. How could she expect him to understand, when she didn't herself?

"Jennie, what's really bothering you? You don't feel guilty because we've made love?"

Numbly shaking her head she found it impossible to look directly into his warm, loving eyes.

"Look, we can't get anyplace if you won't talk this out. At least sit by me on the couch."

They sat side by side, not touching.

"We've known each other such a short time," Jennie said.

"Every minute I've spent with you has been tremendously important. You know that, don't you?"

She nodded, finding it almost impossible to put her feelings into words. "Meeting you has changed my life."

"For the better?" he asked hopefully.

"Yes, but maybe I wasn't ready for change," she said solemnly, staring at her feet.

"That can't be true. You're too young to live like a recluse."

"Matt, please understand." She looked up and met his gaze, unconsciously touching his wrist. "My marriage wasn't just unsuccessful . . . it was a disaster. Kirk's drinking and reckless racing started after we were married.

Nothing went right between us, and I can't put all the blame on him. I wanted him to succeed at things that weren't important to him. I never did understand what he needed from me."

"Why did you stay with him?" He was taking her very seriously now, holding one hand in his in a firm, comforting grip.

"Because I couldn't make up my mind to leave."

"You still loved him?" He didn't try to conceal his uneasiness.

"No." She shook her head miserably. "No, that was the awful part. I knew we'd married too young and for all the wrong reasons, but I wasn't strong enough to face up to my mistake and start over."

"You're starting over now."

"Am I?" She looked away. "Then why am I so afraid of making the wrong decision? Why can't I make up my mind about whether I saw a man committing a robbery?"

"They're two separate problems."

"Yes, but they're both my problems! I don't have the answers."

"And there's nothing I can do to help?"

She'd never heard him sound so unhappy, and part of her wanted to comfort him and assure him of her love.

"I need time." She felt foolish, but dread of losing him made her reach out, bringing his hand to her cheek and pressing his hard fingers against her soft flesh.

"I need you," he said, responding by taking her in his arms, holding her against his shoulder for a long, silent moment.

Don't need me, her heart cried out; *don't ask for more than I can give, not now, not tonight.*

"You can't send me away," he said. "You feel the same way I do."

Easing her back until her head and shoulders were on the cushion beside him, he leaned over and kissed her slowly, drawing the sweetness from her lips as his mouth eagerly moved over hers. The blouse she was wearing under her pale-blue linen suit was a silky one that slipped apart easily as his fingers groped with the buttons, revealing the creamy mounds of her breasts under lacy bra cups. His hand felt feverish as it slid under the flimsy cloth to finger a hard rosy nipple, but her face was even warmer. The skin above her upper lip was tender and stinging as his kisses grew more intense, demanding the response she was so reluctant to give.

Suddenly he stopped, pressing his face against hers for an instant, then taking his weight from her body, slowly rising to look into her face. A light stirring of air from the open window washed over her, but cool air couldn't touch the fire he'd ignited.

"Come to bed with me."

"Not now—I don't see how I can," she said miserably, trying to ignore the tingling around her lips and the nagging desire within.

"Why not?" He stood abruptly, towering over her, his eyes narrowed with anger. "Why is tonight so different?"

"It's not that. . . ."

"You bet it's not! Damn it, Jennie, you're driving me crazy! Doesn't it matter that I love you so much it hurts?"

"You know it does!" She stood, holding her blouse together over aching breasts and pounding heart, feeling diminished by his furious words.

"I don't know anything right now! Why are you making everything so damned complicated?"

"Because it is!"

"Only because your soul searching and hand wringing make it that way! Maybe the past's more important to you than I am!"

"That's not true!"

She wanted to reach out to him, but his anger compelled her to back away.

"Then prove it! Stop pushing me away!"

"Go to bed with you, you mean!"

"I mean make love. Because that's what we've been doing, lady, whether you're ready to admit it or not!"

"I don't want to argue about it now!"

"I do! It's time to make up your mind!" He stood rigidly, hands on his hips, throwing out a challenge that demanded an answer. "Either you love me or you don't!"

"I do, but—"

"But nothing!" He stared at her with angry eyes, frozen to the spot in his threatening stance. "Come here, Jennie."

"No! I think you'd better go. We can talk tomorrow when we're not upset."

"There may not be a tomorrow for us."

His words were so harsh they frightened her, but she was outraged by his outburst, hurt that he was pressuring her at a time when she felt so unsure of herself. She couldn't make herself take the few steps to his arms, wanting instead to escape, unable to bear the pain and disappointment in his stare. He guessed her intention and blocked the way to her room.

For an instant she was dizzy with longing, seeing nothing but the broad, sheltering expanse of his chest. Then he spoke, his fury and frustration making his voice sound like a stranger's.

"You haven't given me one real reason why we can't be together now."

"You only hear what you want to hear!" she lashed out in retaliation, embarrassed by the hot, angry tears blurring her vision.

"I've heard enough," he said dully, the raw pain in his words more chilling than his anger as he stepped aside, letting her retreat to her bedroom.

Pushing shut the door, she pressed the button in the knob to lock it, but securing her sanctuary wasn't necessary. Matt left, slamming the door to let her know he was gone.

How could she survive the night wondering whether he was gone forever? In his arms she felt like a whole person, sometimes stunned by the fervor of her own longings but always made complete by his love.

Her tears dried, and she tried to convince herself she'd been right to refuse him. When she was with him, her emotions raced out of control and her body shuddered for fulfillment, robbing her of reason. The only choice Matt had offered was to make love or not to make love. A relationship demanded much more, beginning with commitment. Their feelings had pushed them into intimacy without regard for the consequences. Until she resolved her doubts, she couldn't blindly take shelter in his arms; but why did his anger hurt so much?

Long after her lights were out for the night, she could imagine his gentle fingers moving over her breasts and his breath hot on the curve of her throat. In spite of his furious words she was seared by a yearning so powerful it threatened to destroy her self-control.

Twice she got up and walked barefoot through the apartment, reaching for the wall phone in the dark but not taking the final step of begging Matt to come back to her.

Morning found her fitfully dozing, more weary when she awoke than if she'd missed a night of sleep. Matt didn't call that day or the next. By the middle of the next week she had lost hope of hearing from him. With the death of hope much of her newly acquired luster vanished. She did her work mechanically, went through the motions of a daily routine, but inside she was constantly weary, with hardly enough energy to pretend that nothing was wrong. She avoided her more observant friends like Tonya, fearing she'd fall apart under scrutiny. Yet calling Matt again was out of the question. Nothing had changed: she still had to wrestle with her own inner demons, and a reconciliation with Matt seemed like an impossible dream.

"You're not going to let him get away, are you?" Tonya asked in the employees' lounge one day, rather hurt because Jennie hadn't confided in her.

"You make it sound like I've been stalking him."

"You can't expect a good man to fall into your lap while you sulk around."

"I'm not sulking!" She was mad at herself for reacting so strongly to her friend's well-intentioned advice.

"Call it what you like, but my sixth sense tells me you're going to blow it with Matt. Then you'll be the one to regret it!"

"Does your sixth sense tell you Smitzer is sneaking around taking notes while we work? He's probably logging every minute we spend in here."

"This office isn't fun anymore," Tonya said petulantly.

Jennie agreed, but she was to blame, not their supervisor. She was so melancholy people were beginning to avoid her. And next Monday the trial would begin.

Thursday she took a different bus after work, getting off a few blocks from Matt's house. He always worked later than she did, so she could walk past his home without being seen. Telling herself it was silly, she still gave in to an almost obsessive need to see something connected with him. It was all she could do not to go up on the front porch and sit on the swing until he came home.

She walked home, the heels she had worn to work making it an uncomfortable trek. The only thing her pilgrimage had accomplished was to fill part of another long, lonely evening. Even if he'd seen her and called her into the house, as part of her secretly hoped would happen, nothing would have changed.

He was sitting on the top step leading down to her apartment, wearing jeans and a yellow plaid shirt with the sleeves rolled to his elbows. When he wore suits and ties he was an immaculately dressed young businessman, but in denim and an old shirt he was even more endearing. Seeing him again did crazy things to her pulse, and she felt breathless, though not from her walk.

"You're late," he said dryly, standing to let her pass him and descend the steps.

"I've been walking." She opened the door and let him follow her into the living room, stuffy as usual at the end of the day.

He didn't ask why or where.

"I walked past your house." She tried to make her voice sound casual.

"For any special reason?" There was still an edge of anger in his voice.

"Special? I'm not sure."

"Why, then?"

She shrugged her shoulders. "Maybe I missed you."

"That's hard to believe. I can be reached by phone, day or night."

"I'm not hard to reach either."

"Lately you have been."

"Matt, I'm—"

"Don't say you're sorry. I'm not going to."

"I wasn't going to. Do you know, you have an irritating habit of interrupting me!"

"Do I?" He looked slightly surprised. "Maybe it's because I don't like some of the things you've been saying. I'm not proud of blowing up, but I still feel the same way."

She wanted to change things between them but didn't know how to begin. "Did you come here to fight?"

"No, I'm not sure why I came. I have to leave in a minute or two, in case you're worried."

"So soon?"

Was this his way of making their separation permanent? An icy dread made her even more confused.

"A few of us are leaving tonight to see the Tigers play the Yankees. We'll spend the weekend in Detroit."

"Well, it's nice you have bachelor friends who can get away."

"I'm the only bachelor. Married men do get an occasional furlough."

"Well, have a nice time." She tried to sound sincere but failed, retreating into the kitchen, pretending to check her refrigerator for something to fix for dinner.

"Why did you walk past my house?"

"I'm not sure." She closed the refrigerator without removing anything.

"Jennie, will you please give me a straight answer?" He stood, hands on hips, watching her without a trace of friendliness in his expression.

She took a deep breath, facing him and calling forth all her courage to say, "I missed you."

"You're actually admitting it?"

He sounded so skeptical she wanted to shake him. "You heard me," she said crossly.

"Yes." He lowered his voice, his features softening.

"That doesn't mean anything's changed," she said quickly.

"Unfortunately, I don't have time to find out for myself. But I do have time for this."

He scooped her into his arms, wiping the pout from her lips with a long, searing kiss, making her come alive with a desperate need to absorb some of his wonderful, vital zest for life.

Her carefully constructed defenses tumbled like a house of cards, leaving her limp and yearning in the circle of his arms.

"Think about this while I'm gone," he said wickedly, caressing her mouth with his lips and tongue until it took all her remaining strength to cling to him.

"We have the trial Monday," he said, the unnecessary

reminder hitting her like a bucket of cold water thrown in her face. "Just say what you think and don't let it eat away at you."

"Is that why you came here, to bolster my spirits?"

"Partly." He bent his head and gently brushed her lips. "No, that's not true. I came because I had to."

"Oh?"

"I missed you. But I have to leave."

Part of her wanted to beg him to stay. They belonged together, and there was nothing she could deny him if he did. But the stronger part of her knew it was best to deny herself what she most wanted: to lie in Matt's arms again and savor his tender, sensual loving.

"Have a nice time," she said again at the door.

"Can I bring you home a souvenir? A Tiger's cap?"

"No." She smiled at the thought of wearing one. "Matt, I'm glad you came. I don't know what will—"

He laid two fingers over her lips. "I'm glad you walked past my house."

"You interrupted me again!"

"Sorry! Next time I do it, you can penalize me. I'll wash all your windows. I hate that job!"

"Don't be silly." She laughed.

"Do that again."

"What?"

"Laugh. It's the greatest sound in the world." He leaned forward for a swift but satisfying kiss. "I have to go. I'm late." He squeezed her hands, smiled broadly, and was gone.

She covered her mouth with one hand, wanting to preserve the warm, tingling feeling of his lips, but kisses alone couldn't quench her thirst for him. His touch made her feel alive, but there was a flip side to her heightened awareness: her imagination tormented her, forcing her to remember every moment they'd spent together. It promised to be a long Friday and an even longer weekend.

CHAPTER EIGHT

The folder was lying in the middle of her desk the next morning with large red felt-pen letters scrawled across it: *Insufficient evidence. See Mr. Smitzer.*

It was the paper work on the college football star's claim, including his parents' signed statement that he was still a student eligible for inclusion on their policy.

"Well, Mr. Smitzer," she said aloud, "that does it!" Picking up the folder she marched into his office.

Her supervisor was talking on the phone, but she went up to his desk anyway. He was jotting down notes on a slip of paper, and she didn't hesitate about reading them: *half gal. skim, tom. sauce, cheddar, marg.*

"My wife," he said sharply, daring her to say anything after he'd replaced the receiver.

"Sometimes a person has to take personal calls at work," she said, hoping to hear the last of his campaign against them.

"Yes, that's true."

"Most of the people here are very conscientious about paying attention to their work, Mr. Smitzer."

"Did you have a question, Ms. Martin?" He took out a handkerchief and patted his face.

"No, but I think this claim is totally valid." She thrust the folder in front of him. "Their son is one of the best-known college football players in the state. His name is on the sports page all the time in the fall. The company will look silly disputing his student status when everybody knows about him."

The little man's face turned sickly white, then deep pink, and Jennie was sure her job was in jeopardy.

"If you're sure," Smitzer said without any of his usual snap, "act accordingly."

She turned to go but was stopped by his voice.

"Wait, Ms. Martin. I'm not much of a football fan."

"No one expects you to be," she said, "but you're an expert on claims. Mary Jane needs help on the Bigelow case and Sam is in a big muddle on that accident at Leiden's. You could be a big help if you weren't so busy supervising."

She dug her nails into her palms, sure she'd gone too far.

"You could be right." His voice was sad and weary. "Not a day goes by that I don't wish I were back at my old desk. But, you know, we have two children—everything's so expensive these days. And this job pays better."

Not for the first time Jennie found herself feeling sorry for him. "Be nicer to people and they'll do better work," she said softly.

His smile was forced, but there was gratitude in it. "Thanks—Jennie—for telling me about the football player."

She smiled, too, adding, "We've always been a team in this department."

Matt wasn't in town to meet her when she got off the elevator after work, but thoughts of him rode the bus with her. Absorbed in thought she walked right past a blue Dodge parked beside the curb near the walkway to her apartment, not even seeing the woman with salt-and-pepper hair cut in a short, severe style with straight bangs. She was digging in her purse for the door key when she heard her name.

"Jennie!"

She turned to find her mother-in-law descending on her

from the ground level, her face puckered with emotion and her arms outstretched. Before Jennie could say anything, Amanda Martin engulfed her in a hug, wrapping thin, dry arms around her shoulders and pressing their cheeks together. A familiar scent of lavender filled her nostrils, one not unlike the sachet her grandmother used to keep in her handkerchief drawer, and she caught a glimpse of a scrawny, freckled shoulder, bare below a gray sleeveless cotton dress.

"When I heard you'd come to Hopewell while we were gone, I just had to see you," Amanda said warmly, stepping back and taking Jennie's hand in hers. "Wouldn't you know it, first time I get Carl to drive me out to Arizona to see my cousin Ruth, we miss seeing you."

Jennie didn't need to ask how the Martins found out she'd visited her parents; the town was so small, Amanda probably knew what they'd had to eat at the Sunday gathering of her relatives.

"Did you come all by yourself?"

"You bet! I told Carl I'm not gonna sit around that farm all the time. When I get the urge to go, I just get in the car and go."

"Well, come in. You've really surprised me."

"Now, I don't want to interfere with any plans you have," Amanda insisted, looking over the living room. "Isn't that the smoking stand you hauled out of the barn and refinished? Doesn't it look nice in your little apartment!"

"I use it to keep candles, matches, candle holders, things like that."

"Just like you did in Grandpa's house. Now, I'm not going to put you to any trouble. I'll be finding myself a motel room. . . ."

"Oh, no. Of course you'll stay here," Jennie said, trying to sound enthusiastic.

"I wouldn't put you to any trouble."

"No trouble. You can use my room. My couch is really comfortable."

"Well, I won't take your bed away. The couch will be just fine."

Jennie knew Amanda would use her bed, but wished they didn't have to go through a whole routine before she agreed.

Feeling awkward because she hadn't stopped to see her mother-in-law in Hopewell, she volunteered to unload her suitcase from the car.

"I do have a few things in the trunk, if you'd like to help me."

Jennie's discomfort only increased as she helped carry a case of strawberries, a large layer cake, plastic containers of cookies, and three jars of jam into her kitchen.

"I was gonna do these berries before I left home and bring them all ready for the freezer, but my cousin Winnie took sick, so I went to see her before I left."

"I don't have a freezer, only the little one in the refrigerator—" She'd started to call her Amanda, but it didn't feel right. When Kirk was alive, she'd called her Mother Martin and found that awkward, too, saying it as little as possible. There wasn't any good title for a mother-in-law, she realized, and now she didn't really think of the high-strung woman as any kind of relative.

"We'll just do up those berries tonight and pop them into what space you have. That is, if you don't have plans. If you do, please don't cancel them. I'll just stay here and clean them for you."

"I don't have plans. It was nice of you to bring—all this. Thank you."

"I was just so darn sorry we missed your visit. Seeing you is like having a little part of Kirk again." Her eyes got watery, and she sorted through the contents of a black plastic handbag for a flowery yellow-and-blue handkerchief.

"I'll get you some tissues."

"No, no, never mind. I'm fine. Just so darn glad to see you."

Jennie couldn't remember ever having been Amanda's favorite person, but her conscience was making her squirm. Had she been thoughtless in not trying to see the Martins when she was home? Amanda's unexpected visit, her first trip to Burdick, made it seem so.

"Remember when Kirk took you to the senior prom? Goodness, he worked his tail off doing extra chores to earn the money to rent that tuxedo and buy those lovely flowers. Little pink roses."

They were yellow, but Jennie didn't say so.

"How long can you stay?"

"Oh, I don't want to be a bother. You probably have things to do this weekend."

"No, not a thing," Jennie said honestly enough, not mentioning the errands she'd hoped to accomplish.

"I will have to leave in time to be back before dark Sunday. Carl doesn't like me driving after dark. Of course, we have these nice long summer days now. Kirk used to work such long hours in the fields with his dad. I had to give him a talking-to about neglecting his little bride."

His mother knew the highways and bars had claimed Kirk's attention, not farm work. Was this how Amanda had dealt with her grief, by painting a rosy picture that made her son seem like a saint?

"Oh, Jennie, why did it have to happen? He was such a good boy. Always thought of his mother. Remember that bookcase he made me in woodworking class? Hand-rubbed every inch with linseed oil. I keep my collection of glass baskets on it."

"Yes, they look very nice there. What can I fix you for dinner? I have some crab cakes in the freezer, or I could send out for a pizza. Or maybe you'd like to go to a restaurant?"

"Dear, we have all these strawberries to clean. Do you have enough sugar and containers?"

"I'd prefer to freeze them without sugar. I know a nice Chinese restaurant. We'll have dinner, then stop at the supermarket for some plastic freezer bags."

"Oh, you need a little sugar to bring out the flavor. Just a few sprinkles in every bag. Otherwise they'll turn mushy. Kirk used to love a huge shortcake, loaded with real whipped cream, not that artificial stuff."

Kirk didn't like to waste calories on anything that wasn't produced in a brewery, but if her way of remembering things made Amanda happy, Jennie would make herself listen without contradicting her. It was promising to be a very long weekend.

Amanda had been a well-meaning mother-in-law, sharing the things she baked, but not taking advantage of the closeness of their homes to run in and out of her son's house to check on him too frequently. Jennie tried to remember all her kindnesses; she tried not to forget that they'd shared the sorrow of Kirk's death, becoming close as they tried to cope with grief. For the first time she began to suspect that Amanda was carrying a burden of guilt. Did she blame herself for Kirk's reckless habits, for failing to teach him to be more sober and conscientious? Was there something she was seeking from Jennie, either absolution or someone to share her failure? Whatever Amanda needed, her memories seemed far wide of the realities as Jennie remembered them.

Saturday she tried to entertain Amanda, taking her to a market where farmers brought their produce early in the morning, then walking through the mall with her, waiting while she picked out mauve knitting yarn and a catnip toy for her kitten, Breezy, one of a litter born in the barn who'd charmed her way into a softer life as a house cat.

For dinner Amanda insisted on buying and cooking a

pot roast and mashing potatoes boiled on the stove top, making enough to last Jennie a week.

"Kirk loved my pot-roast," she reminisced.

This, at least, was true—when Kirk paid any attention at all to what he ate.

"Did that boy have an appetite when he was growing! But he worked it right off doing chores."

Not after they were married, Jennie thought ruefully, beginning to count the hours before Amanda left. Strange how differently people saw the same person, she mused, but she wasn't thinking of Kirk. A weekend without seeing Matt seemed empty no matter how busy she was.

The phone rang as they were clearing the table after dinner. Amanda was closest and picked it up, looking puzzled as she handed the receiver to Jennie.

"You have company." Matt's voice was deep and throaty, the most welcome sound she'd heard since he'd left.

"Mrs. Martin, my mother-in-law." She couldn't bring herself to say "ex" in Amanda's hearing. "Are you having fun?"

"Going through the motions. Having you here would be real fun. How's everything going?"

"Fine." What else could she say? Amanda's obvious curiosity put a strain on the conversation.

"Well, I guess you're busy. I just wanted to say hello."

"When will you be back?"

"We'll start back right after the game tomorrow."

"Three games in a row?"

"Enough to get baseball out of my system for the season."

"I'm glad you called."

"Then I am too."

After Jennie said good-bye, she could sense the other woman's eagerness for an explanation.

"A friend?" Amanda asked.

"Yes."

"Do you see him very much?"

"We're close friends, that's all." She resented the need to explain, but didn't have it in her to be rude.

"Well, that does surprise me. Your mother never said a word, and after we've been friends all these years."

"Mother doesn't know," Jennie said wearily.

"Oh, well, if you're keeping it a secret, I won't say a word to her. But, Jennie, I am surprised." She looked shocked, her face gray and her eyes unblinking.

"It's nothing serious."

"It seems so soon." Amanda was talking to herself. "Hardly three years. I still can't believe it happened. Why did something like that have to happen to my boy? You two were so happy together, so right for each other."

"Amanda," Jennie said slowly, wanting to deal with her illusions but not sure how. "Our marriage was never very happy."

"Not happy! Oh, Jennie, you don't mean that! My Kirk adored you. He used to say you were the prettiest girl in school."

"But that was in high school."

Amanda seemed not to hear. "His dad was gonna let him build on the south forty, so you two would have a nice new house. Grandpa's house was only temporary. We've got it rented now. That's what we planned to do all along after Kirk was making a go of farming on his own."

"He never would have." Jennie spoke softly, but it wouldn't have mattered if she'd yelled; Amanda wasn't going to accept anything different from her own memories of her son.

"If Kirk wasn't happy, it wasn't because his father and I didn't love him. Being the only boy, we didn't want to spoil him, but, my, how proud we were when he did so good on the football team."

Rebellious but defeated, Jennie listened in agonized silence as a woman she didn't even like described a son who existed only in her own mind. She wanted to argue, to urge Amanda to go on with her own life instead of creating myths about her son, but even if she could shatter her illusions, it might be cruel.

Matt said she had to put things in the right perspective; there was no such thing when a woman wanted something she could never have.

Amanda cried a little and grew quiet. They walked around the neighborhood, then came back and pretended an interest in a television program.

Matt had a mother who wanted the best for her son. What would she say to Amanda? Would she blame Jennie for having failed as Kirk's wife? Would she want the same woman for her own son?

Jennie cried that night, too, stifled sobs that her visitor couldn't hear. Her tears were for Kirk and his parents, for Neil Blockman who might be railroaded into a prison sentence as unjust as Kirk's early death, and for herself because her decisions might injure other people and she didn't want to hurt Matt.

Amanda left in the morning, brushing Jennie's cheek with lips as dry as fallen leaves.

"Now, don't be a stranger," she added after her thanks were said. "You know where we live."

"It was good seeing you," Jennie said, believing that, in a way, it was. They'd never be friends, but she felt more compassion on this third day than she had on the first of the visit.

When Amanda was gone, Jennie took away the neatly folded sheets she'd used and put clean ones on the bed, lying down for a nap and falling into a deep, dream-filled sleep, not waking until early afternoon.

The two dolls she'd bought for her nieces had pouty little smiles painted in bright red and stiff, synthetic wigs, one golden blond and the other a reddish mahogany. Her nieces would love them, and the pile of small garments was growing. She wanted to cut out two gold lamé evening gowns from a remnant, but after pinning on the paper pattern she gave up, unable to concentrate on intricate work. Amanda's visit had left her shaken, as unready as she could possibly be for the trial that started the next day.

Matt might be home by now. If she were to call him, what could she say?

Thinking about him she always saw his smile: warm, witty, and caring. He was a man who belonged where he was; that was no longer true for her. Hopewell, Indiana, was part of a different life, one that now held nothing for her, but she wasn't a real part of the community around her either.

Wandering into the kitchen she stared at the framed black chalkboard hanging by the phone, left behind by her former roommate Meg and so handy Jennie kept it there. A piece of chalk was tied to it by a length of string, and she took it between her fingers and thumb, idly making white lines on the board. The head she drew was a little lopsided, but it had Matt's firm chin-line. The ears she added were definitely his, close to the head with full lobes, and by using the side of the chalk, she managed to suggest the casual way his fine dark hair was swept over his forehead. The eyes were tricky to draw, not big and bulging as she first made them or as narrow as her second attempt showed. Sketching in the lashes and brows she gave up on trying to reproduce his warm, loving expression in flat white chalk. The nose she drew was too big, but by blurring the lines with her finger she made it look better. Naturally she drew his mouth in the shape of a smile, adding even, square teeth and the lines that radiated to the corners of his lips. There was only room to add a shirt collar and the neckline of a crew sweater, but when she was finished, it was at least a recognizable caricature of the man she was afraid to love wholeheartedly.

Impatient with her moody doodling she dampened a square of paper toweling to wash the slate clean, but the door buzzer sounded before she obliterated her fanciful sketch.

"Hi."

He was wearing wrinkled khaki slacks and a navy T-shirt with a *D* in the logo and DETROIT TIGERS in big orange letters with white edges that clashed horribly with his red, sunburned nose. "This is for you. In case the Tigers ever win another pennant."

He handed her a plastic bag and grinned as she pulled out a T-shirt identical to the one he was wearing.

"If we ever ride the tandem again, we'll look like a team," he added, following her into the room.

"Thank you. I've never had one like it."

"I was going to get a batting helmet, but it would be too bad to cover up hair like yours."

"Did you have a nice time?"

"We went across the river to Windsor, Canada, last night. I probably did have a good time. About two A.M. the scene got a little blurry."

"Do you do that often?"

"Our baseball weekend? It's an annual outing. Then in the fall the same group goes to a Lions game." He sank down on her couch with a sigh of relief. "It's fun, I guess. So, you had company?"

"My former mother-in-law. She was in Arizona when I went to Hopewell. I didn't know because I never tried to visit her."

"You spent the weekend feeling guilty?"

Her little laugh was forced. "Something like that. Would you like some coffee?"

"No, but a glass of ice water would be great."

"I'll get it."

Her sketch on the blackboard looked childish, and she

picked up the dampened piece of toweling, intending to wash it away before Matt saw it. She was too late.

"Not bad," he said with more than teasing in his voice. "But are my ears really that fat?"

"No! I was only scribbling. You weren't supposed to see it!" She hurriedly wiped away the white chalk lines, sure that her cheeks were as red as they were hot from embarrassment.

"I'm flattered," he said quietly. "It means you were thinking of me."

"I'll get your water."

"You were on my mind all the time."

She took out a tray of ice and turned it upside down to eject the cubes. Instead of freeing a few, she pushed so hard the whole tray emptied, sending most of the ice scattering across the floor. They bent at the same time, starting to pick up the cold, wet cubes.

Before she could stand and drop her handful into the sink, Matt leaned forward on his knees and groped for her mouth, planting a noisy kiss and dropping a slippery ice cube down the V neck of her blouse at the same time.

She shrieked, stood, and lost her handful of ice before she plunged her hand under her blouse to retrieve the melting cube.

"You're terrible!"

"I am, but I couldn't resist." He couldn't stop laughing either, enjoying her struggle.

"If you think that's so funny!" She scooped up several cubes still on the counter and pushed them under both of his waistbands, avenged when he yelped loudly and turned his back to fish them out.

"You deserved that!" Now she was laughing, shivering from the sudden assault of ice as she tried to pick up melting cubes from the floor.

"I probably did, but your aim is a little too good!"

He dropped remnants of ice into the sink and scooped

her into his arms, backing her against the refrigerator as their mouths collided in a searing, seeking explosion. They were devouring each other, opening and closing their mouths as their bodies shuddered with desire. She couldn't touch or be touched enough, digging the tips of her fingers into his lean flesh under his shirt, moving them down his back, under the barrier of his slacks, filling her palms with yielding flesh, squeezed against his crotch as it swelled against hers.

The button on her shorts went spinning across the tiled floor, and his hands parted her zipper. Then her panties were tangled around her ankles, and she was pushing and tugging at his slacks, freeing his hips as he tripped and half fell, saving both of them by clutching the counter.

"We could get hurt," he gasped.

"I know."

She sank to her knees, pulling him with her, both of them struggling and kicking free of clothing until she braced her back against the floor to meet his first frenzied thrust. From far away she heard the sound of labored breathing, but she was lost in a roaring inferno with lightning exploding deep in the recesses of her body, blinding her to everything but the fury and splendor of the man who could plunge her into this world of colorful sensations.

Stunned, feeling as though her reason had fled, she slowly surfaced, still clinging to him with arms and legs, spreading her lips for a kiss so passionately satisfying it brought tears to her eyes.

Slowly her senses started reacting to the outer world, but she didn't want to lose the magic and wonder of being wildly possessive and totally possessed. She felt his heartbeat under the still-heaving expanse of his chest and delighted in the warm wonder of his body, so strong and yet so gentle, so giving and yet totally fulfilled.

Her shoulder was wet where a stray ice cube had melted

under it, and stretching her leg brought her toes in contact with a cupboard. She could hear Matt's knee creak as he flexed it.

"Oh, wow." He buried his face in the crook of her arm, sounding as befuddled as she still felt. "I've never done anything like that before. Are you all right?"

"I think so." She'd never felt so boneless, weightless, rubbery. "Yes, I am."

"Good." He sat beside her, drawing up his knees and pressing his head against them, the curve of his spine so beautiful she wanted to cry.

"I don't know if you bring out the best or the worst in me." He was almost whispering, forcing her to stay close to hear. "Are you sure you're okay?"

As her euphoria faded, she was anything but all right. What had seemed thrilling moments before now seemed savorless. She'd never had the slightest desire to make love in odd places. She was still wearing sandals, and Matt had socks on.

She stood, hoping he wouldn't look at her, but he did, catching her calf in his hand as she tried to move past him.

"I think I'll take a shower," she said, avoiding his gaze because she felt so awkward.

"I'll take one with you."

"No!"

She broke free and hurried into the bathroom, turning on the water full blast and standing under it, shaking because she was afraid of the intensity of her own desires and the consequences of giving them free rein.

Wrapping a towel around her torso she ducked into her room without seeing Matt, not coming out until her hair was nearly dry and she was fully dressed in dark navy slacks and a bulky white sweatshirt far too warm for a summer evening.

He was dressed except for his shirt, the still-damp hair

on his chest showing that he'd washed with tap water in the kitchen.

"I tried to clean up out there," he said, rising from the chair where he'd been looking at the Sunday paper. "We missed a few ice cubes, but I wiped up the water."

"Thank you."

"You are all right?"

"Please don't ask me again! I'm fine."

"I came here for a reason tonight," he said, slowly approaching her.

"Thank you for the T-shirt." It was still lying on the arm of the couch.

"Jennie, I've never felt like this before. I love you so much I'm a little crazy. I meant everything I said that night, but I didn't want to hurt you, only love you."

She couldn't stop shaking. Even with her arms clutched across her chest she was shivering as much as she had when Matt dropped the ice cube down her shirt. First Amanda had spent the whole weekend reminding her, just by being there, of how she'd failed Kirk as a wife. Now, in spite of her good sense and better judgment, she was near the edge of hysteria. Feelings totally foreign to her nature were torturing her on every side, and tomorrow she had to be a witness with a young man's whole future at stake. Part of her wanted to be held and comforted and reassured by the man she loved to distraction, but defense mechanisms she didn't know she had were making her stiff and unresponsive, locking her soul in a cage of fear and restraint.

He took her in his arms, cradling her cool cheek against the warm, soothing fuzziness of his chest.

"You're shaking," he said anxiously. "Jennie, I'm sorry."

"You have no reason to be sorry." She moved away and turned her back. "I'm just a little nervous tonight."

"A little? You're trembling!" He came up behind and

wrapped his arms around her. "Is it me or that damn trial?"

"Neither—no—I don't know. It's mostly me."

"Listen to me, Jennie. I love you, and not just because you make me do crazy things. I came here tonight to ask you to be with me all the time."

She touched one of the hands resting across her breasts, trying to absorb some of the strength in his hard knuckles and broad, tanned wrist. "I don't know what to say."

"If you feel the way I do, there's only one possible answer."

"I love you," she admitted, knowing it would be an unforgivable sin to deny it.

"Then give me your decision now."

"I need time to think."

"Look at me." He spun her around, none too gently, making her see the eager anxiety etched on his face. "When two people love each other enough, there's nothing to think about."

His timing was terrible. Part of her was yearning to agree to anything he suggested, but she couldn't make a decision when her emotions were tossing around like a rowboat in a hurricane.

"Come live with me," he insisted. "On any terms you like. I don't want to be without you anymore."

"You're asking for a commitment."

"I've already made one to you. Is it too much to want it to be reciprocal?"

"Matt, you're pressing me!" She turned her back to him.

"Of course I am! Jennie, what can possibly stand in our way? We belong together."

"I just need a little time!"

"Is it the damn trial that's making you so hyper?" His patience snapped, leaving his voice raw with frustration and yearning. "Nothing's as important as you and me. If you believe that, give me an answer."

"You're not being fair! You're asking me to change my whole life, to take a chance—"

"On me!" he interrupted angrily. "On our love. It's time to start over, Jennie, unless you are hung up on a ghost."

"That's a terrible thing to say!"

"Your mother-in-law." He didn't say ex–mother-in-law. "Does she have something to do with the way you're acting?"

"No! But it wasn't easy listening to her say 'Why did it have to happen?' all weekend."

"Darling." He took her in his arms, holding her stiff form against his. "You're making simple things complicated. I love you. You love me. That's all that matters. You're the only woman I've ever wanted to be my wife."

"You don't know what kind of wife I'll be. It's not an easy job, and I'm not very good at it!"

"Being married to me wouldn't be a job."

"Please don't ask for an answer tonight."

"When, then?"

"I need time to think."

"I can't understand why," he said miserably. "If I'm willing to take a chance on you, why won't you give it a try with me?"

All she had to say was she would, but the words stuck in her throat. She'd helped ruin Kirk's life; tomorrow she might help ruin Neil Blockman's. Matt wanted her, but did he really know her? Could she be the kind of woman he deserved?

"I need time to think," she said again, wondering if she'd ever find her way out of the tortured maze in her brain.

He walked back to the kitchen where his shirt was lying across the back of a chair. When it was on, he stood in the doorway watching her, his eyes dulled by pain.

"The way I'm reading it," he said dejectedly, "it's no."

Her head was pounding, an ache that spread across her forehead, making her cheeks and eyes hurt too.

"You're not going to contradict me, are you?" His voice was hoarse with disappointment.

"I don't know what to say."

"There's a lot more I could say. Did I mention that your body is so beautiful I won't get tired of it if I live to be a hundred? When I dream about you, I wake up in the night thinking I'll go crazy if I can't touch you. At work I spend more time having imaginary conversations with you than I do thinking about my job. My friends seem dull; the people at work are boring; the whole world is bleak and drab when we're not together. Then, when I come into a room with you, it's carnival time: fireworks and brass bands."

"Don't say anymore," she begged.

"This little apartment is beautiful because you're in it. When you smile it's like the sun just came out, and the stars in your eyes—"

"Please don't!"

"Now you're interrupting," he said grimly. "I haven't gotten to the part where I tell you your thighs are like velvet and your breasts—"

"I'm not going to listen!" She ran to her room, slamming the door and bursting into tears because the person Matt loved didn't even exist. He wanted someone he'd made up in his mind. Someday he'd see her as she really was: dull and insecure, certainly not a love goddess!

He came into the bedroom, baffled but silenced by her tears, watching her from across the room.

"Don't watch me cry."

"Tell me why you're crying."

She shook her head, pressing a wad of tissues against her eyes.

"You don't know or you won't tell me?"

"I can't!"

"I can't," he mocked. "That should be your motto; you can embroider it on a banner and hang it over your door."

"Just leave me alone!"

"If that's what you really want."

Facing him angrily, she forgot about crying. "Why do you have to have instant answers? I'm not a piece of art you can take home and put on your shelf. You know what you want, but you've never even asked what I want!"

"I thought I was talking about love. You didn't need to think it over in the kitchen. You knew what you wanted then, and nothing else mattered."

"You're using that against me."

"No! It was the most exciting thing that's ever happened to me. That's why I can't understand you! You haven't got enough sense to admit you want me."

He was angrier than she'd ever seen him, his lips set in a hard line and his eyes uncompromisingly cold.

"Please leave." She didn't have enough strength left to stand up to his anger.

"I'll see you in court," he said, his voice strained by fury, "and God help Neil Blockman if he has to wait for you to make a decision!"

He was so sure of himself! He was always so right! As soon as the door closed behind him, Jennie thought of all the things she should have said: He wanted to make all the decisions; once he was sure of something, he saw it as an absolute truth. His idea of a discussion was a debate; there had to be an instant winner, and he never doubted he'd come out ahead.

CHAPTER NINE

Now that the trial day had arrived, she was numb with dread, reminding herself over and over that she could do little to influence the verdict. Wanda Ackerman had exaggerated her importance as a witness; Matt's positive identification would decide the jury against her young brother. Jennie envied Matt his certainty, knowing what a contrast it would make with her own unsure statements.

At least she could look like a sober, trustworthy witness. Her navy-blue linen suit was too preppy to be fashionable, but worn with a plain tailored white blouse and white pumps, it was the closest she could come to her idea of a somber, concerned citizen.

The prosecutor's office had asked her to be at the courthouse half an hour early, but she took a bus that dropped her near it with over an hour to wait before the trial was to begin. To kill time she circled the county building on foot, really noting for the first time the polished stone façade and steep steps that ran the length of the courthouse. It was the kind of public structure she'd taken for granted until it involved her personally; now she admired the austere but stately lines and the dignity of the setting on a grassy rise above the street level. Maybe the law would prove to be the same: invisible when it wasn't needed but imposing in its fairness and justice. For Neil Blockman's sake she hoped so.

Inside, broad marble steps, worn into wavy unevenness

over the years, led to the second floor, where her heels echoed in a wide corridor. Outside the high solid walnut doors of the courtroom a self-important young man confirmed her identity and scrawled energetically on a clipboard. She was early.

Everyone who bounded by as she watched seemed full of purpose and confidence. A pair of men in business suits, their thick leather briefcases parked by their feet, were heatedly discussing something outside a door with frosted glass and a NO ADMITTANCE sign. There was an air of industriousness combined with an aura of secrecy that made her feel terribly out of place.

Not wanting to meet Matt in the corridor she went into the courtroom, following the young man's directive and seating herself on a dark wooden bench just behind a rail. Except for the pale-yellow walls and ceiling above head-high wainscoting and green leather seats on the chairs along two front tables, the whole room was furnished and adorned with wood stained and varnished to a deep walnut hue. The bench wasn't comfortable; the back curved away from her spine, and the hardwood seat was going to be a trial itself before the day was over. She stood, in no hurry to begin sitting before she had to.

The judge's bench was high and just as imposing as those she'd seen in movies. Below it a woman in a rust-colored suit was uncovering the table and machine where she'd sit to record the trial. The jury box was easily recognizable: another area enclosed by a railing. Everything in the room was vaguely familiar, since courtroom scenes were common on television, but the atmosphere was intimidating. What was she doing in this antiquated cavern of a room, the ten-foot windows crisscrossed by iron grillwork and round light globes suspended on chains as long as her height?

Like a stage crew getting ready for Act I, the people in the courtroom moved around with muffled voices and worry-free expressions. Whatever happened in the room this day wouldn't affect their lives. Jennie wished she could share their attitude, but she saw her role in the proceedings as a heavy responsibility.

The attorneys took their places, the defendant was brought into the room by a uniformed officer, and the cast of characters was almost in place, with the exception of Matt, who still wasn't there. She turned around several times to confirm his absence after Mr. and Mrs. Garber sat down beside her.

Everyone stood. The judge entered briskly, a black robe swishing around his lean form, seated himself, and rapped the gavel. Jennie sat when the others did, glancing over her shoulder just as Matt came in, slightly tardy but looking nonchalant. Neither of them would be called upon until a jury was selected.

Until then she'd avoided looking at the defendant; now all she could see was the back of his head, the straight, dull-brown hair trimmed much closer than in the lineup, not touching the collar of his white dress shirt or tan suit jacket. Had his sister added to her load of debts to buy him a new outfit for the trial?

Matt was sitting at the far end of her bench with the Garbers separating them. With eyes straight ahead he didn't acknowledge her; she stared at the front of the room, determined not to give him a chance to speak.

The one thing no one had told her was how slowly the process of justice proceeded. Expecting to be catapulted into the limelight at any moment, she gradually realized how long it would take just to select a jury. Beside her Mrs. Garber, looking rather elegant in a violet sheath dress with a matching jacket, was fascinated by the questioning of potential jurors, trying to guess which ones would be dismissed before the attorneys made their decisions.

"She's too motherly," Mrs. Garber whispered to Jennie.

"The prosecutor won't want someone who'll feel sorry for that young crook."

She was right about the dismissal, but Jennie didn't like calling Blockman a crook before it was proven. The morning spent selecting the jury seemed long, even though the actual time in session was shorter than her prelunch hours in the office.

The noon break was long too. When it came, Matt stood, glanced in her direction for the first time that morning, nodded with a veiled expression, and left without saying anything. Mrs. Garber invited Jennie to lunch with them, and she accepted, trying to ignore the knot of pain in her throat.

When they returned for the afternoon session, Matt was already there, sitting at the far end of the bench where she'd sat in the morning. The Garbers were walking behind her, so there was no way to avoid sitting next to him without being obvious.

"Jennie," he said woodenly.

"Do you think they'll call us soon?" she asked to cover her confusion and awkwardness, not wanting to think about the stormy, shattering time they'd spent together the previous evening.

"I hope so." He spoke so fervently she wondered if he were nervous too.

"You're eager to get it over with?"

"I have work piled up to my ears at the office," he said gruffly.

A trial wasn't unlike a tennis match, she decided as the afternoon wore on. Each side got a whack at the ball; each attorney had a chance to serve and to return the volley. It wasn't comforting to visualize herself as the ball they'd be attacking.

After opening statements that seemed long and complicated, the prosecution called its first witness, Mrs. Garber. Neither she nor her husband, who testified next, could shed any light on the identity of the thief, but they surely earned the sympathy of the jury by describing how the people in the store were treated and how the jewelry case was looted by a nervous, gun-yielding robber. When they were through, there couldn't be any question that a serious crime had been committed.

Wanda Ackerman, sitting with a chunky dark-haired man in shirt sleeves, was several rows behind Jennie, making her continuously aware of unfriendly eyes riveted on the back of her head. Matt, who'd said almost nothing, kept looking impatiently at his watch.

"The prosecution calls Matthew Todd Nichols."

He walked gracefully toward the witness stand, tall and slender in a heather-gray suit tailored skillfully to fit his broad shoulders. With a calm, serious expression and a steady, low-pitched voice, he took the oath, then settled back in the chair to await Prosecutor Keith Simons's interrogation.

The prosecutor's questions reminded Jennie of the laborious job of hand-sewing a garment, stitch by stitch. No detail was overlooked; the attorney's questions covered everything from the exact spot where Matt was standing to the last he saw of the thief running out the front door.

There was no denying Matt was a good witness. He remembered details she'd almost forgotten, like the thief pulling the shade and bumping the door with his shoulder to make it close faster. Her own befuddled memories seemed more and more inadequate as he smoothly recounted the whole incident.

"Now, Mr. Nichols," Simons said, pausing for dramatic emphasis, "you saw the man without his ski mask for approximately how long?"

"Only seconds. Maybe two or three."

"Was this a sufficient amount of time to give you a clear unhurried look at the man who then proceeded to rob Garber's Jewelry Store?"

"I'd say so, yes."

Matt was so calm he could have been quoting stock prices.

"Do you see that man in the courtroom today?"

"Yes, I do. He's the defendant, Neil Blockman."

"Thank you. Your honor, we have no further questions at this time."

The lawyer for the defense, Judy Zolmon, was a scrappy woman, perhaps in her mid-forties, tall and willowy with jet-black hair pulled back into a severe bun and owlish glasses she took on and off, using them as a pointer when they weren't perched on her generous Roman nose.

"Mr. Nichols, do you wear glasses?" she asked unexpectedly after some preliminary questions.

"No. I own a pair, but I rarely use them."

The defense lawyer hammered away about his glasses, but Matt wasn't shaken, insisting they weren't necessary.

"You were looking out the jewelry-store window without your glasses, is that correct?"

"Yes, but they're not even required on my driver's license."

"The window in question was a display window?"

"Yes, jewelry was on display in it."

"And were you, in effect, looking through an interior window and an exterior window at a distance of approximately fifteen feet without your glasses?"

"Yes, but I don't—"

"Thank you," she interrupted. "And how would you describe the glass in the outer window?"

"It was curved."

"From where you stood, was it convex?"

"Yes."

"And the man who came through the door stood in an entryway beside that window?"

"Yes."

"Does this chart accurately show your position and that

of the window?" She flashed a white diagram of the store layout at Matt.

"As far as I can tell."

"Would you like me to hold it closer?"

"No, I can see it."

"Were you aware of the distortion caused by the two windows?"

"No."

"But, in effect, you were looking at the man through two panes of heavy glass without your glasses."

"Yes, but—"

"Just answer the question, Mr. Nichols."

The prosecutor made an objection, and there was a muffled conversation between the two attorneys beside the judge's bench. Matt looked directly at Jennie, as though gauging how she was reacting to the defense lawyer's persistent cross examination. She knew only too well her turn was next, but doubted if she'd be able to stay as calm as Matt. She was rattled just listening to the badgering he was taking.

"Now, Mr. Nichols, were your glasses prescribed by an optician?"

"No, an ophthalmologist, nearly ten years ago. I thought they'd improve my tennis game, but they didn't."

"Just answer the question, please," the defense warned.

Matt looked grim but wisely let her continue.

"What was your purpose for being in Garber's Jewelry Store?"

"I was picking up a ring my brother left to be sized for his fiancée."

"Mrs. Garber was getting the ring for you?"

"Yes, she'd just brought it out when the robbery occurred."

"Then weren't you looking in her direction, which was, according to her testimony, behind the ring counter?"

"Not at that moment."

"Something attracted your attention at that exact instant?"

"A moment or two before."

"Would you tell us why you looked toward the window instead of Mrs. Garber?"

"I turned to glance at a very attractive young woman."

"You only glanced in the direction of the window?"

"Actually I stared," he admitted a bit reluctantly. "For at least a minute."

"So, Mr. Nichols, you were preoccupied with a beautiful woman when a man pulled a ski mask over his head on the other side of two windows? Isn't it true that you caught only a fleeting glimpse of him through two panes of glass, one of them curved and therefore distorting, and that your attention was wholly on the woman who stood between you and the window?"

Jennie winced, sure the defense attorney would ask why she had turned to avoid his stare. She wasn't enjoying the way the defense attorney was trying to tear apart Matt's testimony by discrediting him. Part of her was relieved because Neil Blockman was well represented, but it wasn't pleasant to hear Matt's character being doubted.

"To the best of my knowledge," he was saying, "the man I saw was Neil Blockman."

Attorney Zolmon didn't give up, but she'd reached a stalemate with this witness. Matt was sure the thief had a bad complexion and mousy brown hair, characteristics the jury could plainly see for themselves on the defendant. He wouldn't admit to needing glasses, and Jennie knew she'd never seen him wearing them. In fact she hadn't even known he owned a pair.

The only part of the cross examination that seemed to annoy Matt was the question of whether he'd been too busy staring at her to observe what was happening outside.

Jennie didn't know what the jury would make of Matt's testimony, but she still believed he was positive about his identification. If Attorney Zolmon was this devastating with a self-confident witness, what would she do to one who couldn't make up her own mind?

Watching Matt walk back toward the benches she felt sick with anxiety. Never a person who enjoyed speaking up in public, she was terrified of the way the defense attorney attacked witnesses. She didn't want to disgrace herself on the stand by crying like a baby.

"A little rough," Matt said under his breath, settling himself down beside her on the bench.

"A lot rough," she whispered hoarsely, missing what was happening in front of the judge's bench.

"Well, I guess you get your turn tomorrow," Matt said in a normal voice.

"Why?"

"It's too late to begin with you. The judge just adjourned for the day."

"I have to come back tomorrow?" She was weak with relief at escaping an immediate grilling, but horrified that she'd have to agonize over it through another night.

"Afraid so," he said sympathetically.

"You did well."

"She made me look silly over the girl-watching part. At least when you testify tomorrow, the jury will see why I was staring."

"I didn't know you had glasses."

"When they didn't help my tennis game, I put them in a drawer and forgot them."

"How did she know about them?"

"Anyone of dozens of people could have told her. She must have talked to someone who's known me a long time. I told you it's a small town when you've lived here long enough. Judy Zolmon is one sharp lady lawyer."

"One sharp lawyer, period, you mean."

"Unfortunately, yes."

Standing to leave Jennie caught a glimpse of Wanda

Ackerman; she wasn't filing out like the spectators around her.

"His sister's behind us. She keeps staring at me."

"You can't let her upset you. You're not here to hurt anyone, only to tell what you saw or didn't see."

He took her arm, walking with her past the angry, anxious face of the defendant's sister.

"Let me drive you home," he said.

"You usually work later than this. Don't you want to go to your office?"

"Work can wait." He held the courtroom door for her, lightly touching her arm as they made their way to the first-floor exit.

"I can take a bus."

"No, I don't want you going back to your apartment alone."

She didn't know how to feel about his protectiveness after he'd ignored her all morning. Being with him wasn't wholly comfortable; too much had happened between them to go on without working out many things. Right now she was too anxious about testifying to think straight.

"Why don't I pick up some Chinese food on the way?" he asked.

"It's too early for dinner."

"Not for me. I raced back to the office to handle a few things instead of having lunch."

She waited in the car while he went into a Chinese restaurant that specialized in takeout food.

His testimony hadn't gone as smoothly as she'd expected; the defense lawyer had scored some points with the double windows and the glasses Matt never wore, but, walking back to the car and driving to her place, he didn't look like a person who was especially upset about Attorney Zolmon's cross examination. He had the relaxed attitude of a man who had done his duty and wasn't worried about the outcome.

"Everything on the menu sounded good," he said, spreading out a bagful of white cardboard containers on her kitchen table.

"It looks like you bought dinner for six."

Did Matt overeat when he was upset? She felt a little queasy watching him heap his plate with two egg rolls, fried rice, sweet and sour pork, pepper steak, and cashew chicken. This was the first time she'd seen him attack food so voraciously.

"You're just picking," he accused her, pausing to watch her push some rice around her plate.

"I won't be able to enjoy anything until this trial is over. I guess for you it is."

"No, I'll be there tomorrow."

"You expect to be recalled?"

"I doubt it, but you didn't think I'd let you face it alone, did you?"

In spite of everything she felt a surge of relief because he'd be there with her.

"I'm glad. But I wish it were over."

"It will be soon. Why don't we talk about us instead? I'm not very proud of last night."

"It doesn't matter."

"To me it does."

She wanted to change the subject; she still wasn't ready to sort out their relationship.

"Matt, I was closer to the window, and I should have seen him better than you. How can I explain that I'm not sure? It will sound like I'm trying to hide something."

"Are you?"

"Of course not!"

"Then be that emphatic on the witness stand." He stood, putting a half-full plate on the counter, and walked to her side, placing his hands on her shoulders. "Don't say anything you don't believe is absolutely true."

"I can't say Neil Blockman is the man. I want to agree with you, but I can't."

He ran his hand over her ash-blond hair, smoothing the crown and flicking a stray lock back in place. His face was out of sight, but Jennie could hear the strain in his voice.

"It doesn't matter if you disagree with me."

"I could be wrong. All I have to offer is doubt!"

"Then that's what you should tell the attorneys who question you."

"You could be wrong, Matt."

"I know, but I don't think I am. Actually I'm a lot more worried about where we stand."

His fingers outlined the delicate curve of her chin, and he stepped so close the back of her head was pressed against him. Disturbed by his closeness she stood and left the table, retreating to stand at the far end of the couch.

"Jennie, put that trial out of your mind. Think about us."

"I'm so uncertain." She was talking about their relationship and the trial.

"You'll do fine in court." He stayed on the far side of the room, speaking in a soft, reassuring voice that didn't completely conceal his own impatience and frustration.

"I'm sorry, Matt."

"You have no reason to apologize. Maybe it's my bad timing, asking for a commitment before you know your own mind. Just tell me when you are sure of how you feel." He moved closer. "I feel like I've been hanging by my thumbs the past few weeks."

"I don't want you to suffer."

"No, I suppose not." He sounded weary and beaten.

"It's not easy for me to make a commitment, not after—"

"Will it ever be possible?"

"You interrupted me again!"

"There are some things I just don't want to hear you say!"

"Starting with the truth?"

"What is the truth, Jennie? I've been trying to figure out your version of it since we met."

"That's not fair. I've never tried to mislead you."

"Maybe not, but you'd better do a little straight thinking before you mess up your life."

"Are you telling me I have to change or there's no hope for us?"

"I'm not trying to tell you anything. I just want some assurance I'm not banging my head against a brick wall."

"Why do we have to talk like this? You're only confusing me."

"Oh, Jennie . . ."

His body seemed to sag, the vitality that was so much a part of him ebbing away. One more crime on her doorstep, she thought bitterly, succumbing to a flood of self-pity but recognizing it as something she hated in herself.

"You've been wonderful, Matt, so patient and kind," she said.

"Forget it. I'm not working for a boy scout badge!"

"Sometimes your attitude is maddening!"

"Make that all the time! I've known what I wanted since you came back from Indiana—maybe even before then."

"Decisions are easy for you. You're always so positive."

"Maybe. I know I don't want to talk in circles anymore. I'm going home."

"Take all that Chinese food with you."

"I'm not as hungry as I thought." His voice was dry and sardonic as he moved toward her door.

"I can't help being edgy!" She wanted to justify herself, but her words came out on a quarrelsome note. "If Neil Blockman is innocent—"

"The jury will make the decision."

"But I may say the wrong thing!"

"I trust you not to," he said, sounding totally drained. "It's time you started trusting yourself."

"That's easy to say."

"Good-bye, Jennie."

"Good-bye," she whispered, wondering if this really was a good-bye.

Their relationship was on such shaky ground, she could almost feel the kitchen tiles quaking under her feet. But he did trust her to testify with integrity. Now if she could only trust herself, the next day's court session might not be such a terrible ordeal.

Matt was upset because she couldn't make the decision to commit herself to him, but in her heart she already had. If there was anything she could do for his welfare, she'd do it, even if it meant giving him up.

She closed carton after carton of Chinese food, carrying them to the refrigerator. Trying to eat any of the well-seasoned dishes would be like swallowing flour paste.

One thing she had forgotten: her supervisor only expected her to miss one day of work because of the trial. Much as she hated to tackle him at home, she had to call.

A child answered the phone in a squeaky little voice.

"Could I speak to your daddy, please?"

There was such a long pause, Jennie was sure the child had laid down the receiver and forgotten to call her father.

"Hello?"

"Mr. Smitzer, this is Jennie Martin."

"How did the trial go today?" he asked.

"Not very well—at least not quickly. I didn't get to testify. I'm sorry, but I can't come to work tomorrow." She held her breath, expecting him to fuss at her.

"That's perfectly all right. There's nothing you can do about it."

"Thank you," she said, rather stunned by his pleasant attitude.

"You've helped me more than anyone in the department," he said sincerely. "Don't worry if the trial lasts beyond tomorrow. You're welcome back whenever you can get there."

"I really appreciate that. Thank you, Mr. Smitzer."

"Clare," he said.

"Clare?"

"Short for Clarence. Good luck on the witness stand, Jennie."

Was that her supervisor, the Mr. Smitzer at the office, she'd just spoken to? Jennie stood by the phone for a long thoughtful moment, not quite believing he'd really appreciated hearing from her what he was doing wrong in his job. It confirmed her faith in telling the truth.

But what should she do when she didn't know what the truth was?

Tonya knocked on her door, a hesitant little tap that Jennie answered immediately.

"Why didn't you use the buzzer?"

"I wasn't sure I should stop."

"Am I glad to see you." She was sad, realizing that being alone wasn't all that great.

"How about jogging? The park's loaded with men lately. There's one who runs every night, six foot six or I'm losing my eye."

"Good idea," Jennie said. It was.

Later, lying in bed, she was exhausted enough to sleep around the clock, but the moment she closed her eyes, the whole scene in the jewelry store started replaying in her mind. What she remembered most vividly was the fear, the frustration of being totally helpless as a jittery thief barked orders and waved his gun.

She was still frightened. If Neil Blockman was the man who'd done it, her own peace of mind was dependent on convicting him. But if he wasn't, she was going to have to live with her testimony for the rest of her life. She might never be certain of his guilt or innocence.

Her last thought before falling asleep was that, without Matt, it was going to be an empty life.

CHAPTER TEN

The air coming through her high apartment window was sluggishly warm already, promising a hot day. There was no reason to dress like an airline flight attendant, Jennie decided, leaving her prim navy suit in the closet and chosing a cooler, full-skirted cotton dress with a fashionably low hemline and billowy sleeves. The natural off-white weave of the fabric was casual, but she'd made the dress from a *Vogue* pattern, which gave it a certain elegance. The only shoes that complemented this dress were high-heeled beige sling-backs, hardly her best walking shoes, but they made her feel taller and more composed.

If she felt as confident as she looked, testifying would be easy. She definitely didn't.

Matt called before she left for the bus stop, his voice brightening her morning in spite of the gloom the trial imposed.

"I forgot to ask last night whether I can pick you up." He sounded a little sleepy, and she could imagine him with uncombed hair and drooping lids, still groggy when he crawled out of bed.

"It's not a problem to take the bus."

"Let me come. I'd like to do something for you."

"All right."

Would the time ever come when she wouldn't want to see him? Even through the pain of their differences he was the source of happiness in her life.

She did hope he wouldn't be late, and not just because she was eager to see him. Her testimony would probably begin as soon as the court was in session. When his car approached the curb, she'd been waiting outside at the top of her stairs for nearly ten minutes, but there was plenty of time to get to the courthouse.

"Good morning." He leaned across the seat and opened the door for her, studying her with steady, serious eyes, darkly shadowed as though his night had been a restless one.

"Thank you for driving me," she said formally, feeling as though she'd been pasted together with glue that might crack or loosen if she relaxed.

His attempts to take her mind off the trial fell flat, and they rode in silence the last few minutes.

"I'll let you off outside the courthouse, then park. Those shoes don't look like they were made for walking."

"They go with the dress."

"I like the dress." He leaned over and touched her cheek with his lips, a ticklish little gesture that was more endearing than sensual.

"I'll meet you inside the courtroom," she said, not wanting to be separated for even the time it would take to park, but compelled to be on time. She didn't want to walk in tardy as he had the first session.

She needn't have worried; they were both early, standing and exchanging a few muffled comments while they waited. The Garbers joined them, excited about the trial and still sure Neil Blockman would be found guilty. Their chatter made Jennie almost sick with worry for the young man, but she also sympathized with the couple because not a piece had been recovered.

The defense attorney was wearing a black tailored jacket and skirt with a pale-pink silk blouse, but the attractive outfit didn't make her look any less formidable than she had the day before. When Neil Blockman was escorted into the courtroom by his guards, Jennie forced herself to look searchingly at his face. Below his drab brown hair his sallow skin was marked by angry red eruptions, seemingly worse every time she saw him. Because his acne problem was so severe, it served as a partial disguise, making it even harder to associate his face with that of the man who'd yanked on a ski mask outside the jewelry store.

The judge entered while everyone else stood, briskly seating himself to begin the day's session. To Jennie his nose seemed narrow and pinched and his eyes indifferently cold. She had no real reason to believe he was bored or cross, but uneasiness sat on her shoulders like two overweight vultures. True, yesterday he'd been soft spoken and fair to both sides, but today he seemed to be her adversary. The majesty of the law clothed him in a black robe; her imagination pictured him as a threat to wishy-washy witnesses as well as guilty defendants.

"You'll do fine." Matt squeezed her hand after they were seated, holding it firmly until her name was called, letting some of his strength ebb into her.

"Your turn," he whispered when she hesitated, not sure she had it in her to make the trek to the witness stand.

"Yes." She moistened her lips with the tip of her tongue, tasting her lip gloss and feeling a little sick.

"You'll do fine," he said again, putting his hand under her elbow to urge her to stand.

After slowly edging sideways to the aisle Jennie started toward the front, feeling slightly dizzy with anxiety. Sure she was on the brink of a catastrophe, she moved forward like a robot. Her feet didn't belong to her; they moved like blocks of ice, the heels hindering her natural movement. One moment she was walking forward, and the next the strap on her shoe shifted, wrenching her ankle sideways with a sudden stab of pain. Stumbling, she saved herself from falling to the floor, but not without attracting attention. Matt rushed forward, offering his support, and for a moment she needed it. Her ankle could be sprained; she could already feel the swelling as a throbbing pain bit into the bone.

"Are you all right?" Matt asked, his arm supporting her.

"Yes, I just turned my ankle." What she really did was fall off her own shoe!

"Can you put your weight on it?"

"Yes."

Everyone in the room was watching her, and she was grateful that Matt didn't say anything about her choice of footwear.

"I'll walk by myself. Thanks," she said gratefully.

She moved toward the witness stand, wincing inwardly as she tried to pretend nothing was wrong with her ankle. Now that her time to testify had come, she was going through with it even if her ankle was broken.

Taking an oath to tell the truth she repeated the words absentmindedly, nagged by a feeling that there was something she should be remembering. The prosecutor didn't give her time to think before beginning with a routine question, but she wasn't fully attentive. Between her anxiety about testifying and the pain in her ankle . . . Ankle! Suddenly she was back in the jewelry store, lying on the floor. The thief had stepped on her fingers, but in that moment his ankle had been in her range of vision, only inches from her eyes.

She realized that Mr. Simons had asked her a question, and she didn't know what it was.

"Would you repeat that, please?" she asked, feeling foolish but elated. There was hope for Neil Blockman if he was innocent!

The prosecutor led her through the basic facts of the felony, confirming that she'd been in the store while the robbery was in progress.

"Exactly where were you standing?" he asked.

"By the watch case. That's on the left as you come through the front door."

"How close were you to the window?"

She didn't want to answer his leading questions, not now that she had something really important to say, but all the time he spent gave her a chance to think.

"Now, you came into the store to look at watches. How did it happen that you turned toward the window?"

"A man was looking at me." She glanced rather apologetically at Matt. "I looked away so he wouldn't think I wanted to flirt."

"Were you able to see the entryway leading from the sidewalk to the door?"

"Yes."

"And did you see a person standing there?"

"Yes, a young man, but I have something important to tell you!"

The prosecutor frowned, obviously not wanting her to disrupt his line of questioning. "Just answer the question, please, Ms. Martin."

She tried to be patient, but excitement made her overly eager to share her sudden insight. Mr. Simons established that she'd seen the thief putting on a ski mask; he didn't give her a chance to tell about lying on the floor and seeing his ankle.

"Do you see that man in the courtroom today?"

"I'm not sure about his face, but I can identify his ankle."

Several spectators laughed, the judge banged his gavel for order, and Mr. Simons's face turned an unhealthy shade of red.

"I'm sorry," Jennie said, speaking rapidly so he wouldn't stop her from saying what she wanted to. "When I turned my ankle just now, I remembered something. Maybe I can identify the thief's ankle."

The attorneys approached the judge's bench, both obviously unhappy about her testimony, neither sure whose case it would help or hurt. When Mr. Simons began questioning her again, he insisted that she answer his questions. He was treating her like a hostile witness now, but she had something to say that had a bearing on the case; she wasn't going to be sidetracked.

"Do you see the man who put on the ski mask and robbed Garber's Jewelry Store in this courtroom, Ms. Martin?" He pursed his thick lips, glaring at her as if daring her to deviate from his question.

"I can't tell by looking at his face, but I may be able to identify his ankle, especially if he has a scar."

"Let's stick with what you saw through the window. You looked directly at the thief?"

"Yes, but all I remember is his complexion. He had acne, his hair was brown, and so was his jacket, muddy brown and very dirty. But I saw his ankle when he stepped on my hand. It was only inches away."

Mr. Simons sighed, his shrewd dark eyes assessing her, trying to decide if it was to his advantage to question her further.

"You can't identify the face of the man who entered Garber's Jewelry Store wearing a ski mask?"

"No, but he had a very bad cut on his ankle. It must have left a scar," she blurted out quickly to avoid being cut off.

"Can you say positively that the man you saw is not the defendant, Neil Blockman?"

"No, but—"

"Thank you, Ms. Martin. No further questions, your honor."

Being cut off was frustrating, but she tried to be calm, hoping the defense attorney would take her seriously.

Judy Zolmon had her glasses off, pressing her lip against the tip of one bow, frowning at Jennie, who was too eager to tell what she'd remembered to be upset by the two lawyers' reactions.

"Ms. Martin," the defense began slowly, "is Neil Blockman the man you saw outside Garber's Jewelry Store?"

"I'm not sure, but I remember the cut on the man's ankle."

"Objection, your honor!" Mr. Simons called out.

The two attorneys argued with each other in front of the judge. Mr. Simons definitely didn't want the jury to hear about ankles. Ms. Zolmon looked like a desperately hungry person who had just been handed a sour pickle. If she asked her client about his ankle, then refused to introduce it as evidence, he'd look even more guilty. It wasn't much, but she had to give Jennie's claim a try.

The judge ruled that Jennie could answer questions about the ankle; the prosecutor had opened this line of questioning by asking her to identify him.

"Ms. Martin, describe your position when you saw the ankle of the man in the ski mask."

"I was lying on the floor, face down. So were the other people in the store. When the thief backed up, he stepped on my fingers. He wasn't wearing socks, so I clearly saw a cut, maybe two inches long, on his ankle."

"Was it a vertical or horizontal cut?" The defense attorney was taking her very seriously now.

"Horizontal, right across his ankle bone. There was dried blood and a raw-looking scab there."

"Did it appear to be a deep wound?"

"Objection," the prosecutor said. "Calls for a conclusion."

"I'll rephrase the question," Ms. Zolmon said. "Did it look more like a wound from a pin or a nail?"

"A nail, definitely. It was more than a minor scratch."

"On which ankle did you see it?"

She was ready for that question too. "It was definitely the left."

"On the outer or inner part of the ankle?"

"The outer."

Jennie could imagine how the defense lawyer must feel. If there was a scar on Neil Blockman's ankle, it would confirm her client's guilt. If there wasn't, it could mean the cut had had time to heal. The defense was taking a real chance by making an issue of her testimony, but Matt's identification had been positive enough to convince at least some of the jurors of Blockman's guilt.

Zolmon gambled.

Neil Blockman removed his blue running shoe and his sock and rolled up the leg of his tan suit pants, looking even more woebegone with one bare foot, and walked up to the front of the courtroom.

Closing her eyes for an instant Jennie put every bit of concentration into remembering exactly what she'd seen.

At his attorney's direction the defendant turned sideways and put his bare foot on the edge of the platform in front of the witness stand.

The judge instructed the baliff to look at the foot, but this officer's declaration only confirmed what Jennie saw: Blockman's ankle showed no sign of a scar, neither recent nor old.

"That's not the thief's ankle," Jennie said emphatically, even though no one had asked her yet.

"Ms. Martin, is this the ankle you saw during the felony robbery of Garber's Jewelry Store?" the defense asked officially.

The prosecution made a token objection but was overruled.

"No, definitely not. The thief had much thinner, bonier ankles. With dark hair, a lot more hair."

Even from a distance the people in the courtroom could

175

see Neil's thick, pale ankle, the few fine hairs almost invisible.

The defense attorney asked more questions; the prosecutor took another turn, insisting she couldn't identify an ankle. But she could! She knew now that the windows had given her a distorted view of the thief, making her uncertain about identifying his face, but his foot had been right on top of her hand. She couldn't possibly be mistaken about the thin, dirty ankle of the thief with the highly visible cut. Blockman's ankle was lumpy, thick, and hairless; in her mind it proved he wasn't guilty.

There were murmurs and stirrings in the courtroom, and the judge demanded silence when a few snickers came from the spectators. Jennie had never felt so relieved. Her instinct about Neil Blockman had been right, even when her memory had failed her. But if she was right, Matt had to be wrong. Her integrity had been vindicated, but only at the cost of his reliability as a witness. She looked in his direction but couldn't read the expression on his face.

The trial wasn't over; it was still the jury's decision that counted, but Jennie was totally convinced of his innocence and eloquent in saying so.

Her job as a witness was over; she was finally dismissed.

Limping uncomfortably she couldn't force herself to return to her place beside Matt on the bench. She didn't look at him. The last thing she wanted was to have him think she was reveling in her last-minute flash of memory. Instead of going to the side aisle she hurried as quickly as her ankle allowed down the center one, exiting through the doors at the back of the room. A nearby drinking fountain quenched her thirst, but the closed courtroom doors dashed her hopes.

Matt could follow if he still wanted to be with her; by leaving she wasn't forcing him to admit he'd been wrong. Maybe he thought identifying ankles was too fanciful; maybe the jury would think so too. That was their decision, but she had faith that Neil would be freed. She knew he was innocent.

Her ankle forced her to walk slowly, but no footsteps echoed behind her; Matt wasn't following. She might never know how he felt about her unexpected testimony. He'd come to the trial only to be with her, and now he was definitely staying behind to avoid her.

She reached the street without crying, then let a hot stream of tears wash down her cheeks. Her ankle still hurt, but she forgot it in the pain of leaving the courtroom without Matt. There was no reason for him to stay behind. Part of her couldn't believe he hadn't followed her from the building, but by the time she dried her tears, it was certain he wouldn't.

Reaching the bus stop she felt relieved of a burden but miserable about Matt. Her hesitation and uncertainty had been justified; now she knew her own judgment was trustworthy. Unfortunately it was too late to make a decision about Matt; he'd let her limp out alone, surely thinking she no longer needed or wanted him.

A bus was just approaching and she got on, knowing full well it wasn't the one that went past her apartment complex. It did stop a short distance from Matt's house.

The sun was building the day's heat to an intolerable level, and her ankle hurt. She was emotionally drained, but this time she had to go to him. His front porch was concealed from the street by a high hedge, and the hanging seat on the cool, shaded porch was the most inviting place Jennie had ever seen. Wearily she sat on the edge, then stretched out, glad for the full skirt that enveloped her legs.

Rocking gently, feeling drugged by the heat, she only intended to rest, but too many restless nights, too much emotional wear-and-tear, overcame her. Eventually she wearied of waiting for a man who didn't come and dropped into oblivion, not stirring until a soft hand prodded her shoulder hours later.

The young couple standing beside the swing looked terribly concerned, the woman asking, "Are you all right?"

"I must have fallen asleep." She glanced at her watch, stunned that she'd slept away the whole afternoon. It was after six o'clock.

"You were here when we came home from work, and Tom didn't think you'd moved since then," the young woman said.

"Thank you for checking." She was grubby and embarrassed, even more so when she saw the tandem leaning against the front of the porch. "I rode your bike once with Matt. It was wonderful."

"We love it."

After the couple left, she waited a short while, hoping Matt would come soon. It was past time for him to be home from work if he had gone back to the office. She couldn't stay on his porch all night, and without a key there was no place else to wait. Night bus rides were something she avoided. With a heavy heart and a miserably stiff ankle, she made her way to the closest bus stop.

Because she had to transfer buses, it took ages to get home. It was incredible that she'd slept so long, but a bath and a cold supper didn't do much to refresh her. Drugged by the heat and strain of missing Matt, she still felt intensely weary.

Maybe she shouldn't have left the courtroom. By trying to spare Matt she might have given him an entirely different message. Her sudden recall of the scarred ankle had vindicated her, but the last thing she wanted was peace of mind at his expense. By leaving she'd given him an option: follow and forgive or stay and reject her. But there was always the possibility he didn't see her exit that way; he might think she didn't want to see him again.

Her ankle felt better when she sat and elevated it, but

she was much too concerned about Matt to quietly nurse what was proving to be a minor injury. Unable to sit still she lowered the thermostat so the air-conditioner would cool the apartment; she was too agitated to put up with the cloying heat. Even wearing only a light cotton nightie and a matching short wraparound, she was uncomfortably warm.

Because of all that had happened, she felt certain the next move was hers; somehow she had to approach Matt, but she didn't know how to do it without ruining everything. Their relationship had been on shaky ground before her testimony. How would Matt feel if she'd succeeded in discrediting him with the jury?

What had happened in the courtroom after she left? Not knowing was the best possible excuse for calling Matt. They couldn't talk about their future on the phone, if there was one for the two of them together, but she could ask what had happened during the trial after she left. At least by hearing his voice she'd have some clue about his feelings for her. Even an angry conversation was better than total alienation; she desperately wanted to talk to him.

His phone rang and rang; he wasn't there to answer it.

The Garbers had mentioned their intention of staying for the whole trial, leaving their store in the hands of his retired brother so they could see the outcome of the case against Neil Blockman. Jennie twice dialed their home number as it was listed in the directory, hoping they could tell her about the afternoon proceedings, but there was no answer there either.

Jennie felt stymied, desperately wanting some kind of assurance that she still had a chance with Matt.

Nothing could divert her thoughts; her yearning to see him was painfully acute. It was after nine o'clock, and her attempts to reach him by phone were still unsuccessful. When her door buzzer sounded, she so much wanted it to be him, she was afraid to open the door and be disappointed.

Braced for the frustration of finding someone else there, she slowly opened the door, not quite daring to hope until she saw him.

Matt somberly met her gaze, asking softly, "Can I come in?"

"Yes, of course."

Her thoughts were rushing too fast to put them into words, but elation overcame her fears; Matt still cared enough to come to her!

Closing the door behind him he looked weary and rumpled, still wearing his light sand-colored suit, but tieless with an open collar.

"I wasn't much of a witness," he said soberly. "I honestly didn't realize the glass was so distorting. I must have been identifying the skin problem, not the man."

"You had to say what you thought." It felt odd to be returning his own advice.

"Blockman certainly has a strong resemblance to the real thief, but I was definitely wrong."

"Definitely?" She was beginning to understand. "Is the trial over?"

"You'd know if you hadn't run away!"

"I was sure you'd follow me!"

"Why would I do that when you wouldn't even look in my direction? I didn't think you'd ever forgive me for identifying the wrong man and letting you think you were the unobservant one."

"That's not why I left, Matt. I wouldn't—I'd never—"

"Hold it against me?"

"I only left because I thought my testimony might embarrass you."

"You ran out instead of rubbing it in? Didn't you think I could handle being wrong?"

"You're trying to make me say things I don't want to!"

"I'm only trying to figure out why you didn't stay for the rest of the trial." He rubbed the back of his neck in a gesture of weariness.

"I thought if you wanted to be with me, you'd follow."

"Was that some kind of test and I flunked?" He spoke softly but didn't manage to conceal his agitation.

"No! I didn't mean it that way at all." She tightened the sash on her wrap, worrying one end of the white print tie with her fingertips. The tiny red flowers looked like drops of blood when seen through misty eyes.

"You were great on the stand," he said unexpectedly. "At first both attorneys wanted you to keep quiet."

Slowly a smile formed on her lips. After all her self-doubt and anxiety she had succeeded in revealing the truth. It wasn't wrong to be proud of herself.

"Twisting my ankle made me remember seeing the thief's. I don't know why I didn't think of it sooner."

"Psychologists say everything that's ever happened to a person is locked away in the subconscious. Sometimes you just need the right clue to unlock a hidden memory."

"Maybe it's better that some things remain in permanent storage," she said, thinking of Kirk.

"You can't continue berating yourself with the past, Jennie. Don't you want to know what happened in court? The jury made the decision." He stepped closer, not touching but caressing her with his gaze.

"So soon?"

"They went out late this afternoon. A friend who works at the courthouse called me at my office when they came back. It didn't take them long to reach a decision."

She held her breath, afraid to believe in happy endings.

"The verdict was not guilty," Matt said solemnly.

"They released him?"

"Yes, thanks to you."

"Oh, wow, I don't know what to say."

"I say well done, Jennie Martin!"

"But that means the real thief is still loose."

He laughed, a light, unforced sound. "Leave it to you to worry about that."

"He might try to rob someone else."

"He might—and sooner or later he'll get caught. So far none of the stolen jewelry has been discovered. When it is, you may get to be a witness again."

"Oh, no!"

"I think you can handle it."

"Much better than this time. I felt so inadequate."

"As it turned out, you weren't," he said sardonically. "I was."

"I didn't want you to be wrong."

"I won't pretend it's not a blow to my ego." He managed a small smile. "But there was never a time when I didn't think I was telling the truth."

"Everything about Neil Blockman fits the real robber: his coloring, his age, his complexion—"

"Jennie, you don't need to gloss over my mistake! I can live with it. I wouldn't want an unjust verdict. I made a serious error, but I've learned a lot from it."

Standing still on her ankle made it throb, but she sat down as a reflex action, hardly aware of the pain.

"You're the most compassionate person I've ever met," he said, sitting beside her and taking both hands in his. "I've never met anyone who cares more what happens to people."

His words were wonderful, but the loving gleam in his eyes meant even more. It allowed her to see herself as he did. She did care about others; it wasn't indifference on her part that had caused Kirk's death. If she'd seen a way to help him straighten out his life, she would have done it. He died because of the way he chose to live his life, not because she was inadequate as a wife.

"What are you thinking about?" Matt challenged gently.

"Kirk."

He frowned but didn't release her hand.

"There was nothing I could have done to prevent his accident."

"That's true. There wasn't."

"I can trust my own judgment."

"I trust it." He touched her cheek with the back of his fingers.

"I don't know how I would have gotten through the trial without your support."

"You would have, but please don't stop needing me at least a little."

Gathering her into his arms he tested the willingness of her lips, parting them with the tip of his tongue and slowly drawing them into a deep, breathtaking kiss.

Stopping before she wanted him to, he held her against him without speaking. His unusually quiet mood told her one thing: the ball was still in her court.

"I went to your house when I left the courthouse."

He studied her, keeping his hands on her arms. "You knew I wasn't there."

"Yes, but you had to come home sometime. I fell asleep on the swing. The couple with the tandem woke me up."

"I haven't been home since this morning. How long did you wait?"

"Until I realized you weren't coming home after work."

"Why, darling?" He covered her lips with his finger, then moved it over her chin, down her throat, under her loose night garments until it rested between her breasts, creating pleasurable ripples of desire.

"You don't have a monopoly on mistakes." She covered his hand with hers to keep it against her skin.

"Oh?"

Faltering, she didn't know how to ask if the offer to share his life was still open. Trying to reach out to him, she released his hand and ran her finger down the press line of

183

his suit pants where it was stretched flat over his thigh, cupping his knee and using the bony hardness to steady her galloping emotions.

"I've thought a lot about what you asked me," she said.

She could feel the tension in his leg as her fingers grasped the swell of his thigh, needing something solid, something that wouldn't slip away.

"Have we wasted enough time?" he asked in a vibrant, passion-laden voice.

"Yes. We have."

Covering her mouth with his he made their kiss a promise, solid and long-lasting, not erasing the past but pushing it into the background, paving the way for their future together.

"No more doubts?" He held her close, whispering against her throat.

"I never doubted you, only whether I could make you happy." She rained tiny kisses on his face, nuzzling his cheek, cuddling even closer.

"You had to make me unhappy before you could decide?" he teased, taking the sting out of his words by kissing her again and holding her close.

"It wasn't like that!" She pulled away but not far away.

"I'm going to ask you one question," he said, "and there's only one right answer."

"What if I give the wrong one?"

"You'll be sentencing me to cruel and unusual punishment."

"That's unconstitutional!"

"A federal offense. Don't you want to know why I didn't come home when you were waiting?"

"Why didn't you?"

"I was knocking off a jewelry store."

"Don't kid about a thing like that!"

"I'm not. I made the Garbers open their store after hours especially for me and hand over this."

He took a square box from his jacket pocket and displayed it on the palm of his hand.

"Jewel thieves get long sentences." Her pulse quickened; this time she was going to tell the truth, the whole truth. . . .

"I expect to get life," he said, snapping open the lid on the burgundy leather box.

The ring was dazzling, a brilliant diamond in a white gold Tiffany setting.

"Life is a long time," she whispered.

"Not long enough to be with you. Are you going to marry me?"

"I don't know what to say."

"Just say yes."

She did. "Nothing could make me happier than being your wife."

"It's about time you admitted it!" He took the ring out of the box and slid it on her finger.

"It fits perfectly."

"If not, I'll have it sized."

"Oh, no. From now on you stay out of jewelry stores!" She threw her arms around his neck, kissing him with joyful enthusiasm, burying her fingers in his soft sable hair.

"I do some of my best girl-watching beside jewelry cases." His hand slid under her nightie, following the satiny swell of her hip, caressing the slenderness of her waist, and reaching upward to fondle her breast.

"You'll be marrying a maniac," he warned, inhaling the clean herbal scent of her freshly washed hair. "In court, even while you were testifying, I remembered how soft your thighs are when you—"

"Don't just talk," she interrupted teasingly, guiding his hand until his fingers brushed silky hair.

"And the way your nipples—"

"More talk!" She slid out of her wrap and lifted the nightie over her head, bringing his hands to her breasts.

"You keep interrupting—" he started to protest.

Her laughter was a joyous outburst of sheer happiness. "I love you. I really do love you!" she said, hugging him against her.

"Interrupt anytime to tell me that."

He led her to the bedroom, turning on the overhead lights as they went through the doorway and pulling the shade before taking her in his arms to press heated kisses on her shoulders and breasts.

"Stand still," she murmured, sliding his jacket from his shoulders and padding barefoot to the closet to hang it symbolically beside her clothes.

"Your ankle is swollen. You should put heat on it." He watched her with more than diagnostic interest, hurriedly shedding his own clothing without taking his eyes from her slender, curvaceous form.

"Later."

"Much later." He pulled her down on the bed with him, celebrating their love with whispers and caresses. She reached up, her hands small but strong, holding his happiness and hers without quivering. Blowing gently she created a miniature windstorm that whipped the whorls of hair on his chest into new patterns, then outlined them with her fingertips, sliding down his torso until he moaned with urgency.

Her breasts tingled, aching with pleasure when his tongue bathed the roseate tips. Lying still under his playful loving was a delight; writhing, responding, reaching out for him, made her longing too acute to be endured.

Love engulfed her like a tidal wave, wiping everything out of her consciousness but their fantastic voyage. Rising and falling on waves of passion she was seared by lightning and shaken by deep rumbles of thunder, but never so lost in her own sensations that she didn't revel in the pleasure she could give the man she loved. In exploring the depths of their love they discovered the heights of happiness.

"I was so afraid I'd fail you," she admitted shyly, curling against him and nuzzling his throat, loving the scent and texture of his skin.

"You could only do that by leaving me." He buried his face against her shoulder, trailing languorous kisses down the length of her arm.

"I'll never leave you. You're stuck with me." She held her ring to catch the light from the ceiling fixture, sorry she couldn't reach beyond the hard surface to touch each glowing blue-white facet. "I've never seen anything more beautiful."

"I have." He planted a lazy kiss on her earlobe, then bent to fill his mouth with her breast, filling her with renewed longing.

"Someday I'll be old and wrinkled," she teased.

"You'll be a beautiful grandmother."

"You're rushing me!"

"I have our future all planned."

"Oh, no, you don't." She scrambled to her knees and held him flat on his back with both hands, trying to scowl but not quite succeeding. "I can make decisions too."

"You don't like to," he teased.

"Maybe that used to be true, but—"

"Used to be!"

"You interrupted me again. It's your worst habit."

"If I do it again—"

"You will!"

"Probably."

"It's a good thing I love you."

"Yes," he murmured, smiling broadly, "a very good thing."

"We should get married soon."

"Name the date," he challenged.

"Labor Day weekend."

"We'll live together—"

"Beginning right now!"

"In—"

"Your house."

"Who's interrupting now?" he asked.

"Who's making decisions?" she retorted.

"This might work," he said, grinning.

"It will." She kissed away his grin but not the delight in his eyes.

"You're right—again," he said, tumbling her off his chest but not out of his arms.

Now you can reserve October's Candlelights *before* they're published!

- ♥ You'll have copies set aside for *you* the instant they come off press.
- ♥ You'll save yourself precious shopping time by arranging for *home delivery*.
- ♥ You'll feel proud and efficient about organizing a system that *guarantees* delivery.
- ♥ You'll avoid the disappointment of not finding *every* title you want and need.

ECSTASY SUPREMES $2.75 each

- ☐ **141 WINDS OF A SECRET DESIRE,** Deborah Sherwood 19548-9-18
- ☐ **142 MYSTERY IN THE MOONLIGHT,** Lynn Patrick 15991-1-18
- ☐ **143 ENDLESS OBSESSION,** Hayton Monteith 12310-0-19
- ☐ **144 MY DARLING PRETENDER,** Linda Vail 15279-8-11

ECSTASY ROMANCES $2.25 each

- ☐ **462 OUT OF THIS WORLD,** Lori Copeland 16764-7-29
- ☐ **463 DANGEROUS ENCOUNTER,** Alice Bowen ... 11741-0-10
- ☐ **464 HEAD OVER HEELS,** Terri Herrington 13489-7-38
- ☐ **465 NOT FOR ANY PRICE,** Suzannah Davis 16454-0-32
- ☐ **466 MAGNIFICENT LOVER,** Karen Whittenburg 15430-8-25
- ☐ **467 BURNING NIGHTS,** Edith Delatush 10885-3-18

- ☐ **7** *THE GAME IS PLAYED,* Amii Lorin 12835-8-49
- ☐ **19** *TENDER YEARNINGS,* Elaine Raco Chase ... 18552-1-47

Dell DELL READERS SERVICE—DEPT. B1222A
P.O. BOX 1000, PINE BROOK, N.J. 07058

Please send me the above title(s). I am enclosing $_____ (please add 75¢ per copy to cover postage and handling). Send check or money order—no cash or CODs. Please allow 3-4 weeks for shipment.
<u>CANADIAN ORDERS:</u> please submit in U.S. dollars.

Ms./Mrs./Mr. _____

Address_____

City/State_____ Zip _____

Catch up with any Candlelights you're missing.

Here are the Ecstasies published this past August

ECSTASY SUPREMES $2.75 each

- [ ] 133 SUSPICION AND DESIRE, JoAnna Brandon . 18463-0-11
- [ ] 134 UNDER THE SIGN OF SCORPIO, Pat West . . 19158-0-27
- [ ] 135 SURRENDER TO A STRANGER, Dallas Hamlin 18421-5-12
- [ ] 136 TENDER BETRAYER, Terri Herrington 18557-2-18

ECSTASY ROMANCES $2.25 each

- [ ] 450 SWEET REVENGE, Tate McKenna 18431-2-10
- [ ] 451 FLIGHT OF FANCY, Jane Atkin 12649-5-11
- [ ] 452 THE MAVERICK AND THE LADY,
  Heather Graham 15207-0-34
- [ ] 453 NO GREATER LOVE, Jan Stuart 16377-3-28
- [ ] 454 THE PERFECT MATCH, Anna Hudson 16947-X-37
- [ ] 455 STOLEN PASSION, Alexis Hill Jordan 18394-4-23

- [ ] 1 *THE TAWNY GOLD MAN*, Amii Lorin 18978-0-35
- [ ] 2 *GENTLE PIRATE*, Jayne Castle 12981-8-33

Dell   At your local bookstore or use this handy coupon for ordering:

DELL READERS SERVICE—DEPT. B1222B
P.O. BOX 1000, PINE BROOK, N.J. 07058

Please send me the above title(s). I am enclosing $_____ (please add 75¢ per copy to cover postage and handling). Send check or money order—no cash or COD's. Please allow 3-4 weeks for shipment.
<u>CANADIAN ORDERS:</u> please submit in U.S. dollars.

Ms./Mrs./Mr_____

Address_____

City/State_____ Zip_____

You'll never forget LAURA.

Her story is one of "almost unbelievable pain and almost unbelievable final joy."*

NO LANGUAGE BUT A CRY
Dr. Richard D'Ambrosio

TWELVE-YEAR-OLD LAURA HAD NEVER UTTERED A WORD in her entire life. Beaten and tortured by her parents as an infant, she had only narrowly escaped death. But her psychological scars were so deep that her very existence was tantamount to a living death. Without speech, without joy, she remained locked in her own world, far beyond anyone's reach. Until Dr. D'Ambrosio arrived. Profoundly touched by her story, he made it his mission to find the way to help her.

*Silvano Arieti, M.D., noted psychiatrist and author

$3.95   LAUREL

At your local bookstore or use this handy coupon for ordering:

Dell DELL BOOKS   No Language But a Cry (36457-4) $3.95
P.O. BOX 1000, PINE BROOK, N.J. 07058-1000   B1222C

Please send me the above title. I am enclosing $_____ (please add 75c per copy to cover postage and handling). Send check or money order—no cash or C.O.D.'s. Please allow up to 8 weeks for shipment.

Mr./Mrs./Miss _____

Address _____

City _____ State/Zip _____